Geneva's Cross

Geneva's Cross

Tammy D. Thompson

Pen & Publish
Saint Louis, Missouri

Published by Pen & Publish, LLC., USA

www.PenandPublish.com
info@PenandPublish.com

Saint Louis, Missouri
(314) 827-6567

Print ISBN: 978-1-956897-07-4
e-book ISBN: 978-1-956897-08-1
Library of Congress Control Number: 2022901121

Cover design by Randi Gammons.

Author photo by Donna Jackson.

Printed on acid-free paper.

DEDICATION

This book, *Geneva's Cross*, is dedicated to a woman who was memorable to me from the first time we met. To the sweet, Geneva Nettles, you inspired this entire story by the way you carry yourself and do all you can to touch others with the love of God. You spread a positive spirit with your faith which is refreshing to see in this day and time. You are unique, energetic, unpredictable, crazy, colorful, and Godly all rolled up into one, and I appreciate you from the bottom of my heart. Thank you for giving me a character people will learn from and one who will lead them to Christ. Thank you for showing me that there is someone out there who cares about others and is always willing to lend a helping hand. Even on days when you aren't feeling the greatest, you still jump in to help. Geneva, you're one of a kind and you have decorated my life with many blessings. I am honored to dedicate this book to you. Keep being the "you" God intended you to be and you will continue to touch lives. I know you touched mine. I love you.

Acknowledgments

There are many I feel the need to acknowledge in my writing journey, especially in this book. First and foremost, I'd like to thank my God, my Savior, for leading me and giving me every thought and every word written in this story which inspired me as I wrote it. God gave me this story and I hope the message is conveyed to every person who reads it.

Thank you to my husband Tony Thompson for always understanding my desire for words, books, and everything that comes with it. You are a rock in my life and a blessing beyond words.

A very special thanks to D.J. Resnick. He is not only a friend but was one of the first people who helped me get started in my twenties when I didn't know what I was doing. Still, to this day, he continues to give his heart and all of himself to my dreams and anyone else who needs the help. Thank you, D.J. for being the mentor I needed then and still need today. I love you.

I want to thank Miss Geneva Nettles for giving me an incredible, inspiring, and energetic character in this book. Your faith and love show everywhere you go, and you have a positive impact on everyone you meet. Thank you for inspiring me from the first time we met. You are truly a blessing in my life.

Thanks so much to my mom, Betty Holder, and my dad Luther Holder, for being my two biggest cheerleaders. Mom, thank you for always keeping my writings when I was a kid, knowing they were special. Dad, the faith you passed down to me, has been an invaluable gift I'll treasure always.

Thank you both for the example you gave to me when I was growing up and into today as well. I wouldn't be who I am without either of you.

To my brother, Jimmy Holder, I'm proud of who you are. You followed God's plan for you and I'm proud to say I'm your sister.

To my son, Cody Thompson, I am proud of you. Through mishaps, mistakes, regrets, and more, we found forgiveness, do-overs, and in the end, love. Let faith guide you through every moment of every day.

I want to thank my good friend, great writer and, as I call her, my *"Event Mom,"* Patty Wiseman. Thank you for believing in me, always being there for me, and for helping to get this book ready to go, editing and teaching me things I had forgotten along the way. You will always hold a special place in my heart.

Lastly, I want to say thank you to my friends. There have been a few I've lost along the way whom I miss dearly, but the ones remaining are true and a blessing in my life. Connie Thomason, Melissa Klitz, Brenda Holder, Terry & Sherry Larey, Cheryl Williams, Charlie McMurphy, are only a few I treasure. Thank you for always being there to listen and support me in my endeavors, no matter what they may be. It means more than you know.

CHAPTER ONE

Elijah peered into the distance, trying to see the future in some mystical place amongst the fog across the clearing over the nearby hillside, focusing so intensely. It seemed like viewing a place far away, yet so close at the same time. All he could hear was the distant echoes of birds as they flocked together to find shelter for the winter soon approaching. Other than that, the whistling wind seemed the only sound, blowing what little hair he had left. Age had taken its toll without a doubt. His happiness little, and worries much, but at the end of the day, his bad choices, or bad attitude, caused it all. *How did I get to here,* he thought to himself? *Standing in this beautiful place alone, but it didn't have to be that way. Dear Lord, I wish I could go back...I can still see her on our wedding day.*

Memories flooded his thoughts like the opening of a dam, drowning everything in its path. Yes, there were things he could be grateful for, but so many regrets kept him bound in chains from past mistakes that made way for his own emotional destruction. People always say you can't go back and look ahead, but he couldn't see what there was to look forward to. Life seemed to fly by like the flash of lightning, there then gone.

"Dad," a sweet voice rang out. "What are you doing out here? It's getting colder. I don't want you to get sick."

"Just thinkin' Ella," still gazing into the distance as the fog got thicker on the ridge.

"About what? Let's go inside and think. You know I've never been fond of the cold dad," she said, shivering like it was below freezing although it wasn't. Her long flowing blonde hair twisted in the wind like a mini-tornado and her striking blue eyes kept on her dad as he stood there like a statue. Caught up in the moment he needed, a pure reflection of himself and his one and only true love, Geneva, took him over. The things he had done made him think he would never see her again.

To say she was a spitfire, full of energy and spoke her mind, wouldn't even scratch the surface of who she was. Her infectious smile contagious and her joyful laugh would ring throughout those hills and echo back, filling it completely. There had been something about her from the first time he met her.

"Come on dad," Ella said, supper is about ready. "Caleb is watching over it right now, but you know he's not much of a cook. If we don't want blackened chicken, we better head that way."

Without a word, Elijah turned, gave a half-way grin, and nodded. He knew he would go back when she wasn't tracking him down and to be one with the nature he loved so dearly, the place that calmed his nerves and took him back to another time.

She held onto his arm making sure he didn't stumble as they made their way down the hill to the old Victorian style home not far away. A little rundown, it needed to be repainted and some porch rails fixed so no one would fall into the flower beds below, but other than that it was fine. Her mom and dad bought it years ago and the wood floors still made their creaking noises when you would step on certain boards, but it had character. The one thing Ella loved the most, was the porch that wrapped clean around it, inviting to say the very least. She caught herself thinking back to good times when they would all gather out there, singing songs and just spending time together. Her dad had never been much of a Christian man, but it seemed he enjoyed the singing of hymns and old songs.

Elijah and Ella Walked into the kitchen and Caleb was standing at the stove trying to stir everything at one time, looking like he was about to lose his mind.

"I got it, honey," Ella said, taking over the task of finishing supper. "Thank you for watching it."

"I'm a chef you know," he raised his eyebrows comically. "But I'll let you finish. I want to make sure you feel needed."

Ella grinned, humoring him, "I appreciate that."

Elijah took his spot at the table, tore off a paper towel, and set it down. He wasn't all that hungry, but he couldn't let on to that. He wanted Ella to know he appreciated her coming to take care of him. She didn't have to, and he knew it. As for Caleb, he was a character. His ways were nothing short of Godly. He carried himself in a way that made Elijah want to be him. Caleb was always quoting scriptures whenever he felt it was needed in a situation of stress or sadness. And, although Elijah never acknowledged it, those scriptures were just what he needed at the time.

"Here ya go pop," Caleb said, carefully placing his dinner in front of him. "Just what the doctor ordered. He said you need to start eating better. You're gonna blow away if you don't."

"I eat," Elijah replied abruptly. "When I want to eat, I eat."

"Maybe you need to *want* to eat more often dad," Ella chimed in, her smile glancing his way in a very uplifting manner.

"Maybe I will."

"Well," Caleb said. "I know I'm gonna eat. I'm starved."

It was funny him saying that because he wasn't very big at all. Now he was tall and wore a beard that was neatly groomed, but he wasn't the least bit fat. You would think so if you ever watched him inhale all the food he did. Where it all went, no one knew, but he ate what he wanted and never gained a pound. There were lots of folks who only wished they could do that, especially the lady who lived just down from him. She didn't eat much, but what she did eat, went straight to her hips. She always came by flirting with Elijah, but it did her no good. He only had eyes for one woman... Geneva.

They sat there and made small talk for a while as they ate the meal, baked chicken, baked beans, potatoes, and fresh rolls. Ella always tried to make sure everyone ate well. Caleb took much of the conversation talking about his dream to write a children's book. He had an imagination without a doubt, and everyone knew one day his dream would come true. He wasn't one to give up on anything he would shoot for. That's one thing Ella admired about him along with his faith in God.

"I think I might turn in," Elijah said, rising to put his plate away.

"I got it, dad. Why don't we sit on the porch for a bit first? We don't do that anymore. I miss it. I remember lots of good times out there."

They put their plates in the sink, letting the washing wait until later, and went outside. In the left corner of the front porch sat a porch swing Elijah made years before with his own two hands. It was perfectly crafted with beautiful etchings across the front seat and on each armrest was a cross. The cross was very detailed and unique to say the very least.

Ella and Caleb sat in the swing and Elijah sat in the white wicker swivel chair to their left, where he could see out into the hillside. Ella's fingers began to run over the cross where her hand was resting, letting the many memories from the stories behind that cross, rush in. She knew the story but wouldn't dare to talk about it. Caleb took her other hand and held it tight giving the smile he always did. It was his silent way of saying *I love you and everything will be okay.*

The wind continued to caress the trees and the flowers in the bed beneath them. Ella made sure she had on a jacket since she got cold so easily, but it was nice. They didn't talk at first. They just enjoyed the symphony of nature God was giving them right then and there. The dirt road leading from the house to the main road had a swirl of dust winding around. Taking in a deep breath and out again, Ella turned to Elijah. "It is beautiful out here dad."

"Was more beautiful," he muttered.

"God outdid himself when he created this place. I don't think I've ever been anywhere more peaceful," she continued.

"Peaceful…uh, lonely is what it is," he said. "And when you two leave…"

"We're not going anywhere dad," Ella replied quickly.

"You can't stay here forever. I did this to myself. You're not to blame and you shouldn't be punished."

"Punished…for spending time with you?" Ella retorted.

To ease the moment, Caleb quickly broke in. "You know it says in the bible not to worry and not be anxious. I know that today you feel this way, but tomorrow is a new day. He has a plan. It's not our plan, but it is perfect."

"Perfect…" Elijah raised his voice. "Perfect for who? You have each other. Who do I have?"

Before they could respond, Elijah pushed himself up out of the chair and shuffled to the front door, slowing before he opened it. There was a pause, and it was as if the wind stopped blowing for a moment, a deafening silence. Never turning back to them, he twisted the nob and went inside. The emptiness he felt was wanting to spill onto everyone around him. A part of him thought if he was miserable, then everyone else should be as well, but that wasn't right.

He didn't want to be miserable, and he sure didn't want his daughter to be, but handling his regrets, anger, and sadness was almost too much for him to carry around much longer.

Elijah went upstairs to his room, and the door's hinges made the usual squeaking sound as it slowly opened. On the bed lay a beautiful hand-made quilt of every color in the rainbow, that kept him warm every night. Geneva made it a long time ago, with love in every single stitch. Thinking back, he could remember her sitting in the rocking chair outside on a sunny day, talking about that quilt.

"You know what Elijah, seems like I get this thang done quicker when I've had a good day," she said, steadily working along.

"Why you think that is honey?" Elijah replied.

Geneva stopped for a second with a thinking look about her face, "I betcha because I'm happy. When Ella comes and gives me a hug, it's a blessing. When we spend time talkin'… it's a blessing. When God gives me a beautiful day like this, it's a blessing. And each one of these squares on this here quilt is put together after each of them blessings. You see, God wants us to slow down and enjoy every moment honey,"

"God…"

"You better betcha God. And don't you start that darn mess again. God put us together didn't he…just like I'm puttin' together this here quilt," she smiled, then looked back down at her work. "I won't tolerate no backtalkin' against my God. You hear me?" Geneva said with conviction and sass.

Elijah's mind came back to present time soon after, leaving him peering at that very quilt patched together with nothing but love. Elijah ran his large, somewhat wrinkled hands across it, and somehow it made him feel closer to her. In a way, it connected him to her once more, even if he couldn't see her.

The sun finally faded behind the hills leaving glimpses of orange and reds until it went dark...remanence of the day. As Caleb would say, God's rainbow. Feeling tired, although he hadn't done much of anything, he readied for bed and climbed in under that old quilt. Still stroking it gently and resting his head on the feather pillow, he let out a long sigh.

Each breath got slower and more relaxed until he found himself where he truly wanted to be.

CHAPTER TWO

Elijah was transported in an instant from the reality he desperately wanted to escape, to a better place and time…one he'd never forget.

"Elijah James, what are you doing in town," an old friend of his granddad's hollered out from one store over, waving as if he couldn't see him.

"Pap and maw sent me to get some things for them. You know they don't drive," Elijah answered, loading things up into the shiny 1955 green and white, two-tone Oldsmobile.

"That ole cuss can drive; he just wants everybody to run after him. He's always been that way," the man continued.

"I don't mind at all. It gives me a reason to drive to town in my new car," Elijah grinned, pointing to the car.

"They're lucky to have a grandson like you boy. I need one like that. The one I got is no account. He thinks work is a dirty word. I tell ya somethin'…takin' him out behind the barn would be too good for him."

Elijah listened to his pap's old buddy gripe about his own flesh and blood, just nodding and acting like he was really listening as he eased into the car slowly, waving as he left. He didn't want to be rude, but if Elijah let him… he would go on and on. He was told to hurry and get back home with the groceries. If he'd learned anything, it was to mind. He had a few times out behind the barn himself and didn't want any more.

Elijah drove slowly down Broad St., although there were lots of people walking up and down the walks, his eyes zeroed in on one person. In the middle of a group of girls, was one particular girl who stood out like the brightest star in the dead of night. He didn't know what it was about her, but when he saw her smile, he almost forgot where he was or where he was going. All of a sudden, he felt a small bump and he came to a stop. Finally looking up after focusing on such a beauty, he had run into the car in front of him. He barely hit him, but the man was furious.

Elijah jumped out and went to see if there was any damage. Luckily there wasn't but the man's finger was about lodged up his nose as he swung it around telling him to be careful and that he was probably too young to be driving in the first place. The man got back in his car and sped away.

Then he heard that voice. "Are you okay?"

Turning slowly, it was like being in one of those old black and white movies, love at first sight. Words wouldn't come out of his mouth like he was frozen.

"I said are you okay?" she said, the very one who had caught his attention to make him wreck in the first place.

"Uh…uh…yeah, I'm ok…uh, thank you…."

"Geneva, my name's Geneva. And land sakes you need to watch where you're drivin'. You coulda killed somebody. What was you lookin' at anyway?" she said.

"I was lookin' at…"

"It don't matter anyway. Next time be careful," she said, whirling around and moseying away.

Yelling out to her, "Elijah."

She turned, and squinted eyes and all, "What?"

"I'm Elijah," he announced as if she had asked what his name was.

She stopped, smiled, her beautiful white teeth gleaming, and her sparkling eyes gave a wink, "Don't have no more wrecks now," She paused. *"Elijah,"* and went back to her friends as they continued their laughing and giggling like before it happened.

This was a moment in time he wanted to bottle up and keep forever. Her reddish-blonde curls and ice-blue eyes captivated him. It's like she was looking clean through him. They were hypnotizing to say the very least. He just about forgot what he was doing when he noticed the time.

I've got to hurry back, he thought to himself. *Pap and maw are going to kill me.*

Elijah rested his foot on the gas and traveled fast as he could without the law getting a hankering to pull him over. He didn't want to anger his pap. He was a kind, caring man, but when he got mad, everyone knew to get out of his way. His eyes were blue, but not the normal blue. They were so clear, sometimes it was like you could see clean into his soul. Some kids down the way were afraid of him because his eyes were so very blue. Maw, on the other hand, was tough. She cared for everyone and had her way of doing things. Everyone had their chores, from what my daddy told me. And if the chores weren't done, she was ready to fight.

"What in tarnation took you so long boy? I hope you wasn't tellin' folks in town that's your car. Get you a job and you might have one like that one day. Now, git in here and put them groceries up for your maw. And make sure you put everything in the right place. You know how she is," Pap said, sitting in his old rickety, thread-bare chair, resting his feet on the antique table in front of him.

"Yes sir," Elijah said, nodding and totting everything to the kitchen.

Still wearing an unmistakable grin across his face, Elijah couldn't get the vision of Geneva's out of his mind. He could still see those eyes, the ones that put him in a trans, even if it was for only a moment. Elijah's daydreaming halted what he was supposed to be doing until he was startled.

"Elijah!" a strong voice rang out. "Put that food away like your pap told you. You're supposed to get back home and watch the twins for your mama and daddy while they go out for a bit. You know how you blame kids drive them nutty. And what's with that look on your face. Why you smilin'?'"

"Just happy maw," Elijah said, never losing the beam shining, ear to ear.

"Well, go on next door and do what you're told," she said, going from one thing to another, but not doing much of anything at the same time. "Go on now."

While leaving, he handed the keys over to Pap and did as he was told. The last thing he wanted to do was watch his sisters. They were twins which meant double trouble for him. It always seemed like one day Brenda would be sweet and Bridget would be the one causing trouble and the next, the other way around. I guess it didn't matter really because you couldn't tell them apart except for the mole on the back of Brenda's neck. That's how everyone told them apart.

Elijah went on to his house and he analyzed it as he'd never done before. It was a small white frame house with mint green shutters. The paint was cracking and in dire need of some tender loving care, but somehow it always got put on the back burner. His mama had a few flowers around the small front porch, but there were usually more weeds in it than flowers. She always tried though. Climbing roses had taken over on the left side of the porch, painting the area with vibrant pinks and reds, giving the house a festive presence.

Elijah crossed the lawn and started to go inside, then glanced up and noticed a moving truck across the road a few houses down. Not thinking much of it at first, he had to tackle the task of watching his sisters. Babysitting them was never something he loved doing, but he figured it was what big brothers were supposed to do. He had just turned 17 and they were only 8. He figured his parents must've been a glutton for punishment to want to have a few more kids to raise. Regardless, he was stuck with these two blonde-headed little girls who lived to aggravate him whenever they got the chance, which was daily.

Elijah's parents left. After he got the girls situated, Elijah went to the front porch and sat in the old, faded brown, rocking chair. With every rock backward, the boards underneath, played their tune, interrupting the peace in the air. The sun was trying to sneak away, only to leave the darkness behind. Before the sun was completely gone, he noticed a familiar car pull up. It was parked downtown when he was there earlier. Out hopped someone he was shocked to see. It was Geneva. It was her. She was walking toward the house where the moving truck sat in the driveway.

From the distance, he could tell how beautiful she looked in her white top with fringe around the neck and sleeves, and a hot pink full skirt that bounced when she walked.

I must be dreaming, he said to himself. So, he closed his eyes real tight then opened them again. This time he could hear some conversation from their yard. They had to be yelling or else he wouldn't have been able to hear so clearly. His curiosity started getting the best of him, wondering what was going on down the way.

"Geneva," an abrupt voice called out. "You were supposed to be home an hour ago. We got unpackin' to do girl. Come here."

"But grandpa, I was just..." she said.

"No buts. This is the last time your late girl," a man's mean scruffy voice rang out once again.

The next thing he heard was something he didn't want to hear. Not sure what she was being whipped with, but by her cries, it wasn't good. A part of him got very angry even though he didn't really know her, but he wanted to. Then Elijah went back in to check on the girls. They were content being left alone, so that's exactly what he did. They always did play well together.

"I'll be right back," he told Brenda.

"Where you goin' Eli?" she asked, looking up from her play make up and dolls.

"Just a few houses down, you two stay here. Don't go outside," Elijah replied. "Don't go outside."

"I'll tell mama and daddy you leave us," Bridget said in a nagging kind of way.

With a half grin to her and pat on her head, he went back outside. Unsure of what he was going to do. He felt like Geneva needed him. He got an uneasy feeling and couldn't let it go. It got darker, and he stepped carefully down the walk, being guided by the streetlights. When he reached her house, he slowed down, almost stopped. The lights inside were dimly lit and there was no porch light. Then he could hear something over by the bushes to the left of their front porch. It sounded like crying.

Taking a deep breath, not sure he should even be there, Elijah eased across the street and made his way toward the sound.

"Geneva, is that you?" he whispered, getting closer to the sound.

CHAPTER THREE

"**P**op," a voice rang and was shaken at the same time. "Breakfast is ready."

He opened his eyes to find Caleb standing over his bed, smiles as usual, waking him from a dream he wanted to stay in. He wanted to see her face again.

"Why did you wake me?" Elijah said angrily, then rolling over and covering his head up. "I need to go back to sleep."

"But it's after 9 am. Aren't you hungry?" Caleb asked respectfully.

"You stay hungry enough to eat for the lot of us, so eat mine too. I want to sleep," he said, covering up his head with that quilt, so he could find the same place and time he was pulled from.

About then, Ella poked her head around the door to his room. "Come on dad, I made all your favorites. Homemade hashbrowns, crispy bacon, homemade biscuits...gravy."

"Can't I just sleep?" he begged; his head still covered as if to tell to say *leave me alone*.

Ella motioned for Caleb to leave, "We'll be downstairs when you're ready to eat. I'll keep it warm for you dad."

When the door shut, he flung the quilt off him and began to have somewhat of a tantrum. Not one for people to see or anything like that, but one he needed to get out all his frustrations. Then he reached into the nightstand to grab his glasses when he grabbed something else along with them. It appeared to have been wedged in the crack of the drawer sitting almost upright.

Putting his spectacles on, so he could see what he had, the envelope was dusty, and flap sealed. There was no writing on the outside, but it did have a beautiful fragrance coming from it. He would know that scent anywhere. Just taking it in, made it feel like Geneva was sitting right next to him.

Elijah knew Ella and Caleb were waiting on him, so he placed the envelope back where he found it and went downstairs. But after breakfast, he knew the first thing he was going to do, open the letter. So, he went downstairs to join Ella and Caleb.

"There you are sleepyhead," Ella said, finishing her plate and getting his from the microwave where she was keeping it warm. "Did you sleep okay?"

"Great," Elijah responded quickly, thinking about it all over again. "I dreamed of your mama. And I'll tell ya something. That's one dream I didn't want to wake up from."

"That's why…" Caleb started.

"Yes," Elijah interrupted. "That's why I wanted to go back to sleep."

"You know it's almost impossible to pick up where you leave off in a dream dad," Ella said, serving him breakfast. "I read that somewhere, but it never hurts to try, I guess."

"Well, you can betcha I'm gonna try again tonight," Elijah replied, his attitude glaring.

Silence filled the room momentarily then Ella's look turned from all smiles, to more solace. "You couldn't have known dad. It wasn't your fault."

"I wasn't nice to her like I should've been," Elijah lowered his head. "Always more worried about me and what I wanted to do than what she needed. I don't know what I was thinking Ella. What was I thinking?"

Ella, realizing there needed to be a change in mood, "I remember when I was really little, mama always sang that song *This Little Light of Mine*, every night before I would go to sleep. From an early age, I knew she had a light like I never saw in anyone else. There was always something about her smile that lifted me up even when I was at my lowest."

"Yeah," Elijah half-smiled. "You know I've never been much of…what you would call…uh, a religious type. But I swear that woman always made sure I knew the way to go if I ever wanted to be. She told me lots of times *Elijah, I ain't givin' up on you and neither is God.* If I heard it once, I heard it a thousand times."

"Nothing wrong with that Pop," Caleb muttered, holding a mouth full of eggs and biscuits which were about to fall out.

Ella and Elijah looked at one another, then back at Caleb, and burst out laughing at his usual antics. One thing for sure, he never claimed to be anyone but himself and everyone loved him just the way he was.

"What?" Caleb said, working hard to swallow his food.

For the first time in a long while, Elijah found some laughter, even if it was from Caleb's lack of manners and natural humor. They all knew a lighthearted moment was needed. Elijah, getting very nostalgic, letting memories flood his brain, sat there with a somewhat peaceful look.

"Hey," Ella jumped up. "Why don't we take a little drive today. You know dad, get out of here for a while and do something fun."

"Well, uh."

"Let's do it Pop. We all deserve it," Caleb chimed in a spirited way. "We've been hanging around here too much. We need to get out of the house. It'll do us all some good."

Letting out a long sign, Elijah looked at the two of them gazing at him with begging eyes, waiting for an answer, "I guess we could, but I don't wanna be home late."

"We won't be dad," Ella said, clapping her hands with joy. "I just thought we might drive to Hot Springs for a few hours, maybe walk around and shop."

"Shop?" Caleb and Elijah said in unison.

"You bet," Ella laughed. "Now you two get ready. Let's go on a road trip."

They never saw her clean that kitchen up in such a hurry. The drive to Hot Springs was about an hour and a half, but the scenery would take your breath away. All the winding roads and mountainside views approaching the city always gave a feeling of peacefulness. The sprays of a dozen different colors would melt together creating a perfect rainbow of nature in every direction. That's the one thing Elijah remembered about such a scenic drive. And since Hot Springs wasn't too far away, that's where most people in those parts went to getaway.

It wasn't long before they were all loaded up and Caleb took the wheel. Putting on the unusual hat he always wore, his smile lit up the car. He acted like he was going on an adventure.

Caleb always tended to have a heavy foot and Ella kept an eye on him, making sure the law had no reason to give them special attention with those blue lights. He would glance over to her every little bit when the speedometer would rise a little. And it was amusing to say the very least, but nothing could get Elijah's mind off the letter in his nightstand. How could have not seen it there as many times as he opened that drawer, he never knew? It didn't matter anyway. It would be late afternoon before they made it back home, so he had to make the best of the day.

They made it to Arkadelphia and turned toward Hot Springs. Ella always wanted to stop at the little shops between the two. There were all sorts of places selling antiques, yard décor, and just nick-nacks. Long as Elijah could remember, Ella always loved those things. To be honest, she liked to shop…period, but the unique items caught her eye the most. She was just like her mama when it came to that. Geneva loved to stop at little places and brought home the darndest things. She'd say *it's different just like me, honey!*

Although most of the time Caleb did as Ella wanted, he didn't in the least, want to meander around and not have anything in mind to buy. Before reaching their destination, on the right was a very interesting place. To say it was colorful, would be an understatement. From metal animals in the front to rows of flowers on the side of the building, it was hard to miss. It hinted of much more inside.

"Caleb stop there." Ella quickly yelled out, grabbing his arm, almost turning the wheel. "There."

Caleb, thinking he'd dodged the *shopping* bullet, didn't, and giving in to her sudden request, they pulled to the side of the place and parked. Ella's giddiness overflowed, grabbing her purse, and jetting out of the car before anyone else. Caleb and Elijah just looked at each other, shaking their heads and following her.

"Don't wait on us," Caleb whispered with a slight chuckle following.

"You know better than that son," Elijah remarked, getting out of car slowly making his way into the store.

Ella roamed aisle after aisle touching everything. There was something about women and shopping, making them touch everything, whether they intended on buying it or not. Ella was no different. She did that from the time she knew what shopping was. Mesmerized by the array of hundreds of interesting things encircling her, Ella's attention was taken, and impossible to veer her away. From little trinkets to hand-knitted Blankets and everything in between, her eyes were taking it all in. The place smelled like a combination of Cinnamon and vanilla, mixed with a hint of old. You know, there's a smell of old, and it surely found its place. With so many things, no one could look at it all in a day, but Ella sure wanted to try. Her gazes went up and down, left to right, making sure not to miss a single thing.

Caleb stood around the door until his wife had enough of that ancient stuff surrounding them. He knew it could be a while, but like he told Elijah once, patience is one thing he had plenty of, and with Ella, patience was needed.

Elijah got bored and decided to walk around to see if there was anything to catch his eye. More than likely, there wasn't, but it was better than standing there with Caleb twiddling his thumbs. Besides, sometimes treasures get found in the most unlikely places. Elijah began walking, feeling a little gritty sand under his boots rustling around on the concrete floor beneath, as he did so. A lot of things were a blast from the past to him. On one shelf, sat an old forty-five record player. You could tell it had been there for a while, looking at the thick dust covering it, and next to it lay a stack of albums. He remembered many good times listening to those old 45's when he was young, but times change, and things were far different than they were back then. He thumbed through the albums to see if any were familiar to him, then glanced up for a moment. Something else caught his eye on the other side of the shelf, something making his heart flutter momentarily. And he hurried around to the other side.

CHAPTER FOUR

L aid across a black felt piece of cloth, sat something spec-tacular. The small cowhide cross with beautiful etchings and a small turquoise cross set dead in the center, left Eli-jah spellbound. First, he didn't dare pick it up, but his eyes stayed focused in just the same...causing his mind to travel in time.

Suddenly, Elijah's memory traveled to where his dream left off the night before, taking him to Geneva once more.

Elijah crossed the street where he could hear crying. The closer he got, the more he saw Geneva sitting up against the side of the house with her knees pulled to her chest and her arms wrapped around them. It appeared she was rocking back and forth slightly, her head lowered and hiding.

"Geneva, is that you?" he asked, whispering, still slowly walking in her direction.

"Go away," shewing him away. "He'll see you."

"Who?" Elijah remarked, looking to see if anyone was watching. "It's Elijah from earlier in town...you know, the wreck."

Slowly getting up, she leaned over to keep from being seen by whoever she was hiding from and met Elijah on the other side of the bushes. They sat down on a small patch of grass, and, for a moment, silence took front and center. Crickets sang their songs as each night before and lightning bugs were flying all around, like tiny lanterns lighting their way. The slight breeze cooled down the warm evening and, at first, Elijah didn't know what to say.

"Are you okay?" he asked, wanting to put his hand on hers, but not knowing her well enough for such. Still, the thought made him go crazy.

"I'm fine, but I hate him," Geneva replied, an irritated look showing.

"Who?"

Geneva glanced back at the house and a tear found a path down her cheek, "My grandfather. He's mean...just plain mean. I want to find my mama."

Confused about what she spurted out so quickly, "What are you holdin'?"

Something rested in her hands which she held tightly and then to her chest like she was afraid to let it go. She rocked back and forth for a moment, and it appeared she didn't know if she should open up more than she already had. Then she lowered her arm and opened her hand.

"It's a cross," Elijah said. "So what?"

"So, what?" she said almost angrily and standing up to leave.

"No, wait," Elijah said apologetically. "Why the cross?"

She sat back on the grass, and lifted it carefully, smiling, "My mama...my mama gave it to me when I was little. I know it's kinda different since it's part leather, but I always did love it. Turquoise is my favorite color. Mama said when she saw it, she thought of me. Well, what happened with her is a long story, but I find peace in it, Elijah. It tells me God's always got me. Even in times when he's grandpa is bein' mean. Gods got me."

"Can I see it?" he asked, slowly holding out his hand. She placed it in the palm of his hand.

"Long as you give it right back," giving a small hint of a smile but with attitude at the same time.

His fingers ran over the smooth parts of the hide and the parts with cool etchings and designs. But in the middle was a beautiful turquoise cross, the perfect size to fit in your hand.

"Okay that's enough, give it back," Geneva barked. "God might think he's supposed to help you instead of me, but I hope he helps you too. Don't get me wrong. I wouldn't wish bad on nobody."

Elijah handed the cross back, "God don't even know who I am."

Time in Elijah's mind fast-forwarded quickly when Ella walked up to him, still standing in the same spot. Her eyes shimmered like diamonds as she was engulfed in a place holding so much history, secrets, and treasures.

"Dad, I found the absolute most perfect..." she started to say, only to find him gazing ever so carefully at that small perfectly imperfect cross on the shelf in front of him. She put her hand on his shoulder, and he seemed a bit startled but snapped out of it soon after.

"What'd you say, Ella? I'm sorry, I was..." Elijah said, finding his way back to the present.

About then, she reached in front of him and picked up the cross. "It's beautiful. It reminds me of..."

"Yes, I know," he interrupted. "I know."

"I'm buying it, dad," Ella said, turning and starting to the register.

Elijah Hurried behind her and pried it from her hand, "No you won't. I am," he said abruptly before she could make it to the register.

No words were needed. Their hearts were speaking to one another without a single syllable spoken. They both knew there was something special about the cross. Something about it gave them peace and little more happiness than before. Something about it spoke loudly amid silence.

Ella placed a pair of beautiful hand-painted angels with the name Carolyn Young signed underneath. The talent and heart it took to do such an inspiring pair, showed nothing but pure love. She also found a dream catcher she had to have. The lady behind the counter was elderly, each line showing, but it was obvious she was a happy sort. She smiled at Ella and wrapped the angels in paper to keep them from breaking and put the other in a sack on top of them.

"Will that be all young lady?" she asked, pecking at the old cash register sitting on the glass case.

"Yes ma'am. This is a lovely place," Ella responded kindly, her eyes still wandering around the room in case there was something she overlooked.

"Been here for more years than I can count young'un. Some days I think I shoulda just brought a cot and moved in. Been collectin' all this stuff from decades of folks wantin' to discard stuff that's valuable to others. I guess that's why I'm still here," the woman said.

She said the total of the items and Ella paid her in cash, a little more than asked. The lady gave a sweet *Thank you dear*, then Elijah laid the cross in front of her.

Her age-covered hands, a few fingers crooked from life's work, reached over and very carefully picked up the cross.

"My lands sake," she muttered softly. "Didn't think anybody would ever buy this old cross."

Intrigued, Elijah replied, "Why not?"

"Oh, I've had this cross for many years. I'd like to think I could remember but I do remember the man who brought it in. He was a snide old man who just wanted the money. Didn't seem like he cared about what that cross meant in the first place," she paused. "He just came in and said all it ever did was cause him trouble, so he sold it to me for little a nothin'. Anyway, it's been on that shelf waitin' on the right person ever since. And I suppose it was you."

"It reminds me of someone," Elijah said, once again running his fingers over it. "Someone very special."

"Well, memories are good. When it's all said and done, that's all we got…memories. Hold'em close. I'm alone now. Everybody's gone, but I still got my memories. Thank God for that," she said, a contented smile gracing her face.

Elijah started to say something about God but refrained. He could see her faith in her eyes and hear it in her voice if that's even possible. Who was he to try and squash somebody else's hope? Anyway, it didn't matter. He wasn't sure if he believed in God or not, but there had to be something out there, so he just paid her and thanked her as they left. A part of him felt very sorry for her, but somehow, he got the feeling she was okay. With only a short conversation with her, there was no doubt her life was a good one, filled with love. To be honest, he began to feel sorry for himself. He envied her. Deep down he wanted to feel exactly like her.

Ella grasped onto Caleb's hand and began to swing their arms like kids used to do when they were little. The gleam on her face illuminated all around her and Elijah could do nothing but smile. Elijah's little girl had grown up to be a beautiful, wonderful, and caring woman and for that, he was very thankful.

"Whatcha thinkin' dad?" she said, putting her seatbelt on and getting ready to ride a little farther into town.

"You," Elijah replied, giving a crooked grin.

"Me?" she smiled. "What did I do?"

"Just bein' you Ella…just bein' you," he winked.

"Is that a good thing dad?" she asked, turning halfway around, looking him in the eye.

"It's a great thing. I'm proud of you. I'm proud of who you are, and I know it wasn't because of me, but you are something special," he answered. "Don't ever forget you're special Ella."

"That's the sweetest thing you've ever said to me dad. Well, except for then you were trying to run the boys off when I first started dating. You told me no one was good enough for your little girl," Ella said.

"What about me?" Caleb chimed in as usual. "I'm good enough, huh Pop?"

Once more, he got Ella and Elijah both laughing, not at what he said so much, but how he said it. His character rang clear in his attitude which was always uplifting. His way of saying things came out at odd times and was mostly comical. It's like he knew when laughter was needed, and he obliged.

"Where to now?" Caleb said, a few miles out of town.

"I have an idea," Ella smiled. "Why don't we just stay the night and go home in the morning."

"Oh Ella," Elijah started. "I...."

"I know what you're going to say, dad. You're going to tell me you got lots to do around the house when you know you don't. It's good to get away from home for a bit. It's just one night. Besides, Hot Springs is a beautiful place, and we'll have a good time," she interrupted before he had a chance to give an excuse as to why they shouldn't stay.

"I wouldn't argue with her," Caleb said, grinning. "It's hard to win with her."

"I suppose it'd be alright," Elijah agreed. "But first thing in the morning we go home."

Elijah could tell the wheels were turning in Ella's mind. The look on her face lit up. "Let's stay at the Arlington. It's historic and has lots of character."

"Has lots of ghosts too Ella. I'm not too fond of ghosts," Caleb said, looking terrified of the idea.

"Oh, my goodness. You don't believe all that rig amaro, do you? It's only stories people made up. There's no such thing as ghosts. You're just chicken," Elijah aggravated.

Caleb straightened his shoulders and sat up a little straighter and said, "I'm not scared of anything...but ghosts."

"Let's stay there," Elijah laughed. "It'll be fun to watch Caleb. That'll be entertainment all on its own. What do ya say, son?"

"Very funny pop," he said. "Just wait until you see I'm right. I bet you'll be running out of there with your tail between your legs just like me before it's over."

"Geneva and I stayed there once," he said. "When we were young. It was a beautiful, majestic place. And there was no talk of ghosts back then. If there had been, I promise Geneva would've been outa there. With all her bible talk, there was no room for paranormal anything. I can promise you that."

"That's because the ghosts hadn't moved in yet," Caleb's voice shook. "But I bet they live there now."

Finding another belt of laughter from Caleb's point of view on the subject, Ella held her belly, she got so tickled. All the while, Caleb slowly drove toward the downtown area, straight for the hotel.

"Have you heard the stories Pop?" Caleb started again. "You had to have heard the stories."

"What stories son?" Elijah replied, waiting to hear something ridiculous coming from his lips.

"They say Al Capone used to rent out the entire fourth floor of the hotel for his crew, bodyguards, and gangsters. And there's a tale that if you get on the elevator, it mysteriously opens at the fourth floor even if the button wasn't pushed like it's letting someone off," Caleb said like he truly believed such stories in the first place.

"That's what it was Caleb," Elijah laughed. "A tale. Surely you're not really scared."

Ella wasn't saying a single word but chuckling the entire time. His humor, unique, but Caleb truly believed everything he was saying. His tone let out lots of color regarding the old stories he heard, and they came out like the truth.

Slowly making their way downtown, driving past the stores, gift shops, the wax museum, and much more, directly in front of them sat the old building which had stood the test of time.

CHAPTER FIVE

"There it is," Ella said, excitement presented in her voice. "I hope they have a room available."

"I hope they don't," Caleb whispered below his breath.

Majestic, it stood as before. Two of, what appeared to be bell towers, one on each side above the entrance of the hotel. The oval-shaped awning over each window going on each side of it, were stately, showing the age of the place. The stairway up to the front, still grand, but the past showed a little in every detail.

When they got out and headed inside, Elijah remembered clearly the only other time he ever stayed there. It was his and Geneva's honeymoon. They had driven to Hot Springs since they couldn't go much further than that with the little money they had, and that memory became his present time momentarily.

*

"Elijah honey, this is beautiful," Geneva said, clutching onto his hand.

"Not as beautiful as you," he complimented, walking inside.

The cathedral-type ceilings and marble floors were a sight to behold. Geneva couldn't help but fill her eyes with the beauty surrounding the two of them. Every detail magnified in the eyes of a small-town girl who was country to the core.

"This is too much," she said, kissing Elijah on the cheek and looking around once more.

They walked up the counter to get checked in and had to wait a few moments for another couple to finish.

*

"Elijah," a voice said.

"Yes dear," he replied, then turning to notice who he said it to.

"Dear," Caleb gave a funny smirk. "You got a new name for me now Pop?"

"Never mind," Elijah snapped, wanting to finish his thoughts. "What?"

"Do we only want one room or do you want one by yourself? I wouldn't recommend it...you know everything we talked about," Caleb said seriously.

The lady behind the check-in desk, looked at them a little funny, although she probably knew exactly what they were talking about, and gave a slight grin, trying to act like she wasn't listening in.

"Makes me no difference. I'm not a scaredy-cat," Elijah replied confidently, nudging Caleb in a playful way.

"One room please," Caleb told the lady. "Two double beds."

"Yes sir," she replied. "Typing a few things than grabbing two big skeleton keys. You'll be in room 439."

You would have thought she threatened to throw him off the highest mountain, play Russian roulette, or such. His face turned white as a sheet and started to show lots of anxiety instantly.

"Any other rooms...floors," he asked quickly.

"No sir," she said, looking back at the screen. "We've got a conference going on and all other rooms are booked up."

"We'll take it," Ella answered, pushing Caleb away before he denied the one room they had left.

"But...," Caleb tried to continue.

"We'll take it," Ella said once more before he could spit out something embarrassing.

Elijah, still thinking about the past a little, couldn't help but laugh at him. The lady handed them the big key and Ella thanked her politely while Caleb already looked like he'd seen a ghost. Watching Caleb was like watching Abbot and Costello in the haunted house. For a moment, they could almost hear his knees knocking together.

"Enjoy your stay," The lady said with a smile.

"That's easy for you to say," Caleb muttered.

Hitting him in the arm, Ella kept her pace toward the elevator not far away. Caleb walked in slow motion, trying his best not to follow her. He acted like he was headed to his doom.

They got in the elevator and pushed the number four, and it was nothing short of amusing watching Caleb squirm. And when the door opened at their floor, they had to pull him out.

"Come on," Ella said, grabbing him by the arm. "This is childish."

Caleb didn't say a word. He just kept his eyes down the long corridor leading to room 439. It had a somewhat musty smell, and you could tell the carpet had been there for quite some time, but it was nice. The doors were half solid, half louvered.

"This is like that movie *The Shining*," Caleb said, trailing behind them. "Don't you think?"

They reached the room and opened the door with the unusually large key and went inside. The décor was nostalgic, a flashback in time without a doubt, and Elijah went over and sat on one of the beds.

"Are y'all ready to go explore?" Caleb said in an anxious manner.

"Alright then," Ella agreed. "Let's go before he has a coronary dad."

Elijah, only along for the ride, nodded. They spent the day in town going in and out of shops, the museum, and then stopping at Granny's Kitchen to get a bite to eat before settling in for the night. It was a quaint little place. The outside had a simple red awning and, in the window, were handwritten specials including Cobblers for dessert. It was perfect considering Elijah was sweet on sweets and Caleb would eat just about anything.

They went in and the simplicity of the place magnified but made them feel right at home at the same time. The bright yellow counter and wood shelving across the wall filled with nick-nacks caught their attention right off.

They found a table and the waitress came right over. Her friendly nature was inviting. She appeared to be middle-aged and wore a contagious smile. She took the orders and hurried to the kitchen. The folks already there, looked like they were probably regulars because the waitresses knew all their names and knew what they wanted to order.

It wasn't long and she brought out the plates, full to the brim, no room left for anything else.

"How's it look?" the waitress asked, placing the last plate down in front of Caleb.

He didn't even take time to answer before he started digging in. He acted like he hadn't eaten in weeks, but then again, that was every meal for Caleb. The expression on his face showed he was pleased with the sustenance picked for supper.

Ella spoke for them all, "Incredible. Thank you."

"Y'all let me know when you get ready for dessert now," she said, hurrying to wait on someone who just came in.

"Dessert," Caleb said, looking up momentarily, then steadily shoving his dinner down his trap until it looked like nothing had ever been on his plate in the first place.

The sun was beginning to go to bed for the night, only a hint of light peeking out. It didn't matter though, because the hotel was only a few blocks away and the walk would be nice. As they got finished up, the waitress came back over with the ticket.

"Whenever your ready folks, I'll take care of that. By the way, where you folks from?" the waitress asked.

"Texarkana," Ella answered. "Not too far away."

"Where y'all stayin'?" she continued. "Lots of nice places around here."

Caleb couldn't wait to answer that question, "The Arlington."

"Ohhh," she said, pausing. "Beautiful place…although my superstitions run away with me and I'm a little scary."

Elijah laughed out loud and added, "Caleb is too."

"I've heard stories, but then again, they could just be stories. Anyway, it's been here a long time. Lots of history. Well, I hope you enjoyed your meal. Come back to see us." she said, scurrying away.

Ella paid the bill and gathered her bags of things she bought throughout the day, and they started back to the hotel. They hadn't walked a few stores down when they saw one of those *Zoltar* machines with the sultan-looking figure inside that's supposed to tell your fortune.

"Hey," Ella said excitedly. "Let's do it, Caleb."

Ella drug Caleb to that crazy machine, and it was steadily saying, *"Give me a quarter and I'll tell your fortune."*

Ella put her coin in and the figure in the machine began to move. His mouth opened and closed several times, and a piece of paper came out of a little slot in the front of the machine.

"What'd it say?" Caleb said.

"It says *Look forward, don't look back.*"

"Let me try," Caleb said, shoving his hand in his pockets to dig out a quarter. "What's my fortune?"

Once again, Zoltar began to move around, mouth opening and closing for a moment and a piece of paper came out for him as well. Ella and Elijah never knew Caleb was so superstitious but being there brought it to light.

"Let's see," he said, glancing down at the small slip of paper, but he wouldn't read it out loud.

"What?" Ella said. "What does yours say?"

Caleb balled it up and dropped it on the ground, "This is a scam...who believes in this stuff anyway? I don't. Let's go."

He went ahead, trotting quickly, but Ella stopped and picked up the small roll of paper he just discarded. Caleb still walking, opened it, and started to laugh.

"Come on dad," she said, tickled by what she read.

"What did his say?" Elijah asked curiously.

Ella showed it to him. It read, *someone, is watching you, be careful.* It was all Elijah could do to keep from falling over laughing. Caleb was almost a block ahead of them by that time and stopped to look back. All he could see was them smiling ear to ear and holding back how funny it truly was he got that fortune on that day. If he hadn't been scared before, he was then.

They caught up with him and Ella linked her arm with his, "I'll protect you, honey."

"You are so funny," he responded, looking straight ahead. "You'll see Ella."

They crossed the street and walked up the steps to the hotel, and the people from the convention were heading outside. With so much to do in town, they were more than likely going to take the town by storm. They walked in and there were a few more groups of people in the restaurant, but few others lingered. Ella dug around in her purse and pulled out the large key going to their room, and they got in the elevator.

There was a couple who got in with them and they pushed floor two. When Ella pushed four, they both looked at her. Not a word was spoken, but you could tell they knew the tales Caleb had been telling.

Ding, the elevator sounded off as the door slowly opened.

CHAPTER SIX

S tepping out, the place had a ghost town feel to it, little noise and no one shuffling in the halls at all. When back in the room, Ella asked Caleb to go get some ice from the ice machine down the hall. He gave her a look of disbelief that she would even ask him such a thing.

"I'm not going by myself," he said, shaking like scooby-doo in those old cartoons.

Ella grabbed the bucket, humoring Caleb, "We'll be back dad."

When they walked out, Elijah went over and left the door barely cracked open so they could get back in, and then he laid the covers back and took off his shoes to get more comfortable. A creaking sound suddenly filled the room, and he went to see what it was.

"Y'all back that quick?" Elijah asked, peeking around the corner, but there wasn't a soul in sight, but the door was opened all the way.

Thinking maybe a draft made it open, he shut it almost closed once more, but by the time he walked to the bed, that same sound echoed once more.

"Ella," he said, looking, only to find it opened again.

Maybe Caleb ain't crazy, he thought to himself, shutting it completely. About the time he made it to the bed, an abrupt knocking came at the door, startling Elijah to the point where he jumped.

"Why did you lock us out Pop? Come on, open up," Caleb said erratically.

He let them in but didn't bother mentioning what just happened. He knew if he did, Caleb would sleep outside before sleeping there.

They fixed a drink, talked a bit, and turned on the television. They weren't really watching it, but it filled the space with sound just the same. In case there were ghosts, the noise would drown them out.

"I'm beat," Elijah said, climbing in bed and covering up with the sheet provided and thin, antique-looking comforter atop it.

Caleb walked around the room analyzing every single inch of it. From the curtains draping down to the pedestal sink in the bathroom. He was doing his best to find something strange about it all. Elijah didn't dare say anything about the door opening on its own or he knew Caleb would be gone in an instant.

"Me too dad," Ella said. "It's been a long day. Come on honey, I'm tired."

"Just checkin' things out," Caleb responded quickly, steadily pacing around the room.

Finally, after a few minutes, he settled down and readied for bed. About the time they turned out the lights, a sound of water dripping came from the bathroom. It would drip once or twice, then stop. Then it would wait a minute or two and do it again.

"Did y'all hear that?" Caleb said.

Neither Ella nor Elijah responded, doing their best to get some sleep, he let it go. A few more random dripping noises came and went but nothing else out of the ordinary. So, Caleb relaxed best he could and scooted closer to Ella.

Lying still, Elijah rested his head comfortably on the soft feather pillow, pulling the covers up to his neck since the chill in the room was obvious. He reached and took the cross he had bought earlier in the day and held it close to his heart like Geneva always did. He figured if she believed God would keep her safe, then he tried to believe the same. In a way, holding it, helped him think he was holding her just the same.

Elijah breathed slow, in and out, and all he could think about was the day they had and the memories which surfaced in the middle of it all. Then, the envelope he found in his nightstand, came to mind. He let it play over and over what it could be, what it said, and when it was left there. As all the random thoughts cluttered his brain, the day's activity led his tired body into slumber. A calmness filled every bit of him as his subconscious led him back, whisking him away into a time machine that only his dreams could offer.

He opened his eyes, and he was no longer in the hotel, but home instead, awakened by knocking at the door. "Elijah James," a familiar voice called out. "I know you're not still in bed. If you are, it's just plain ole laziness."

He heard Geneva call out, and it only took him a moment to get up and throw some clothes on. He quickly combed his hair and took one last look in the mirror before rushing to the door.

Swinging it open, trying to catch his breath..."I was up...I was just..."

Geneva pushed her way inside, "Elijah James, you know the Lord will shoot you down for lyin'. Why you're sleepin' the day away? I thought you said you was takin' me to the river to do a little fishin'. It is a might chilly but not too bad."

"Well...uh."

"Speak up," she demanded. "You sayin' we're not goin'?"

"You see...I don't have a..."

"Car," finishing his sentence. "I know. I saw your dad drove it this mornin'. I put two and two together and figured you just acted like it was yours. It's alright though. I have a truck."

"You drive a truck?" he asked since she didn't look like the type.

"You betcha I do," she said, making two fists and plopping them down on her hips. "Guys aren't the only ones who can drive trucks. Truth be known, I can do anything a man can do…well, almost."

She offered an interesting laugh for a moment, and Elijah stood there in awe of her incredibly colorful and unique personality. She had a way of saying things like no one else he had ever met before.

"Well, you got poles?" Geneva said. "We can dig up some a them fat worms down at the Red River and catch us a mess," she continued, more and more energetic as she spoke.

Elijah grabbed a jacket and a few poles from the shed out back, and he followed her to an old red Ford pick-up parked in front of his house. They hopped in and she started it up. At times, it sounded like it might die with all the spitting and sputtering it did, but they made it to their destination in no time. She hopped out of the truck and went to the back, grabbing the poles. She had a small container and a little digging tool as well, picking them up and looking to Elijah.

"Let's find some worms so we can get started," handing him the poles.

She found some softer ground, crouched down on her knees, and commenced digging. Geneva dug into that dirt like she was born doing it, smiling the entire time, like she was in her element.

"Looks like you've done this before," he said, standing with poles in hand.

She let out an entertaining cackle, "You betcha I have. From the time I was old enough to talk, I was digging up worms. Sometimes I did it just for fun. Lots a kids hated the way worms felt, but I always liked them slimy little rascals.

Most times though, we fished for supper. My daddy and I went fishin' a lot before he went into the military."

"What about your mama?" Elijah asked, remembering how she said she wanted to find her.

He noticed he had struck a chord when she didn't answer right away, she just continued putting big ole long worms in the container next to her. Getting the hint, he changed the subject quickly.

"Things better at home with your grandfather?" he asked kindly, hoping to smooth over what rough path he'd just taken.

"Awe, 'bout the same I suppose. He's still as mean as a rattlesnake. Sometimes I wonder if he don't have ice water runnin' through them veins a his. Thank God for this cross I keep with me or I'd a done shot him."

Looking quite shocked, Elijah responded, "Really?"

Geneva stopped what she was doing and sat on a log, "I'll tell you somethin' if you don't tell anyone."

He pretended like he was closing a zipper on his lips, "My lips are sealed."

Well, she carefully started, " My grandfather has always been an ornery ole' cuss. You see he's German and it ran clean to the bone I swear it. Anyway, when I was eight years old, it was my job to butter the biscuits and put them on our plates, so I did. But when it got to grandfather's..."

"What? What?" Elijah said, curiosity welling.

"You see," continuing her story. "I was so mad at him. I had been wantin' to get back at him for always bein' so mean to me...so I went out to grandpa's bug box and got pinch of some white powder. I figured it was poison and that's what I wanted."

"Are you pulling my leg, Geneva? You seem too sweet for something like that," Elijah said, steadily grinning thinking she must be joking.

"You done got me started now, so let me finish," she said. "I took that pinch of poison and put it on his biscuits, then buttered them."

"What happened?" Elijah gasped, more than surprised by such a story.

"Well, you know he ain't dead, don't ya? The old buzzard was so tough it didn't even phase him. He was so mean, every time a dog or cat got in our yard, he would shoot at'em and laugh at how they jumped around if he didn't outright kill'em."

"Now I see why you were crying that night I heard you," Elijah said, slowly easing his hand to rest on hers.

She gave a slight jerk but didn't resist such a sweet gesture. "Well, I have my faith and I suppose that's all I need."

"Where's your cross?" he asked, curious if she really carried it everywhere she went.

She reached into her jacket pocket; there it was. Slightly worn from the constant rubbing, but there just the same. It was second nature for her to caress it the entire time she had it in her hand.

"Why do you do that?" he asked, wanting to get into her head a little more.

"Makes me feel like Jesus is holdin' my hand," Geneva said with a smile. "He's holdin' yours too Elijah."

"I don't know about that Geneva. Like I told you before, I don't think God even knows who I am." Elijah muttered.

"In Psalm 139 Verse 13 it reads '*For you formed my inward parts: you knitted me together in my mother's womb.*' So, you see, he does know you. He created you."

"I've never been a holy roller, to be honest. Not real sure I believe in a higher power. I just know I'm here," he continued the conversation.

She continued her bible lesson, and didn't miss a beat, "It also says in 2 Chronicles 15, verse 2, *The* **LORD** *is with you* *while you are with Him. If you seek Him,* **He will** *be found by you; but if you* **forsake** *Him,* **He will forsake you.**"

"I don't understand," Elijah said, trying his best to decipher what he's not used to hearing. In a way, it was like puzzle pieces he never could put together.

"Don't give up on him and won't give up on you honey," she said, scooping up the worms and treading to the fishing spot just past the trees. "Come on!"

They enjoyed several hours of fishing, although they only caught a few brims and threw them back, but it was the company he liked the most. Something about her rang clear in his heart, drawing him closer to her by the minute. She had her line in the water and it started tightening quickly, jerking her forward. Elijah put one arm around her waist and the other on the pole to help her reel it in.

"It's a big one I think," she said, swaying back and forth. Then all the sudden, the line broke, causing them to fall back onto the ground at the edge of the large bush shadowing them.

Elijah was on his back and Geneva was to his side, his arm still around her. The sounds of the wind through the trees played all around them and their eyes were locked on each other. Their hearts pounding came together in perfect unison. Pulling her closer to him for the kiss he had dreamed of his heart began to race, "Geneva."

CHAPTER SEVEN

Like being ripped out of a movie during the best part, the next thing Elijah knew, he was staring up at Ella, once again in the hotel. "Rats," he said, "not again."

"You talked in your sleep all night dad," she said. "I don't think Caleb slept much either."

"It wasn't because of his talking," Caleb said from the other side of the bathroom door.

"I dream a lot," Elijah replied. "So what? Everybody dreams."

"Let's get ready, go eat and head home," she said, giving a sweet pat on the arm, knowing it's what he wanted to do.

"Sounds good to me," Elijah nodded.

Caleb came out of the bathroom towel drying his hair, looking very relieved to be leaving. His beard had a fluffed look until he combed it neatly like it always was.

"You sleep good Caleb?" Elijah asked, trying his best to aggravate.

"Pop, let me tell you something. This place is creepy. I swear I heard pops and drips and dings all night long. And, at one time, I wanted some more ice, but I was afraid I'd see the ghost of the bellman walking the hall," Caleb countered. "I'm not kidding."

Elijah wanted to laugh at Caleb, but in a way, believed what he was saying. They all finished getting ready and went downstairs to check out. The same lady was behind the counter as the day before. She took the key and gave a kind *thank you for staying with us*. Caleb didn't say anything like before because he knew Ella would really hit him if he did. They just went outside toward the car, but before they reached it, Ella had the idea to go to the same little restaurant as the night before and grab breakfast. She knew if they didn't, Caleb would be wanting to stop not far down the road.

The three walked back into that place, the same waitress who waited on them the night before, came rushing back up.

"How you folks this mornin'?" she asked in a friendly tone. "How'd you like the hotel?"

"Fine," Elijah and Ella spoke at the same time, but Caleb didn't say a word.

She looked at Caleb and grinned, figuring he chose not to answer the question.

"What'll ya have?" the waitress asked, notepad and pen ready.

"I think I want three eggs scrambled with sausage, bacon, hash browns, and huh…biscuits and gravy. Yep, that'll do it," Caleb said, closing his menu and handing it to her.

"Where do you put it all son?" she said, amused, then turning and taking the rest of their orders.

It wasn't long and the food came out. They had their fill of some good home-cookin' style breakfast, something they all grew up on, Caleb rested his hands on his belly, showing just how full he was. His comedic personality always helped keep them laughing.

"There's nothing like homemade biscuits," Ella said. "I remember mama always made the best. She said her mama taught her when she was a little girl. She sure taught her right."

Elijah didn't say a word. Anytime Geneva was brought up, it's like he bottled everything up inside of himself and hid away.

"Well, kudos to the chef," Caleb said, sopping up the last bit of gravy left with the last biscuit on his plate.

"We ready?" Elijah asked, wiping his mouth, and getting up. "We need to be getting back."

Ella didn't argue with him. The fact was, she too wanted to get home. At least for the moment, it was their home. She knew they would stay if he needed them.

On the drive back, there was no stopping anywhere and Elijah laid his head back and slept most of the way. For once, no dreams found their way into his head. For the first time in a while, sleep was sleep. And before he knew it, they were headed down the road to his house. So glad to be home, Elijah looked up and saw a car parked in front of the house.

"Is that…" Ella started saying.

"My sisters," Elijah completed her sentence. "Yes, it is."

"Why I haven't seen aunt Bridget and Aunt Brenda in a long time," Ella said. "I wonder if Uncle Tom and Uncle Jimmy are with them."

"I imagine so. Them four travel everywhere together," Elijah said. "They love their cruises too. But I'm not so sure about being stuck out in open waters like that. I've seen *Titanic.*"

"Oh dad," Ella said as Caleb stopped the car. "I think it would be fun."

"I'm with Pop, Ella. I'm not the best swimmer and I'm thinking you need to be if you take a cruise," Caleb laughed.

Ella ignored their little banter, and got out and headed toward the house, but didn't see anyone. She did, however, hear them inside the house. She was sure they locked everything up, so Jimmy must've remembered where the spare key was hidden underneath the fake rock in the flowerbed.

"I bet I know where they are," Elijah pointed toward the kitchen. "At least Jimmy anyway."

"Behave dad," Ella nudged him, going up the front steps.

When they opened the door, Brenda and Bridget, Elijah's sisters, were sitting in the living room talking. Someone had already started a fire to get the nip out of the air. Tom, Bridget's husband, met them at the door, shaking their hands and hugging Ella.

"You two look beautiful as ever," Ella said going up to her aunts, their blonde hair flowing and blue eyes, unique and stunning.

Elijah went into the kitchen to grab a glass of tea, and there stood Jimmy, Brenda's husband.

"What's up Jim?" Elijah said. "I see you found the spare key."

"We figured you'd be back sometime soon, so we just let ourselves in," he said, eating the little leftovers from a couple of days earlier. "I hope it's okay Eli. We didn't think you'd mind."

Elijah nodded as to say *fine* and sat down at the table after getting a drink. He never knew what Jimmy was going to say. If anyone said his mouth had a filter, they would be completely wrong, but he was a good man. Years ago, no one might have said that considering he had lots of rowdy ways, but it seemed Geneva pushed those scriptures on him enough to where he found the light somewhere along the way. He still didn't lose his aggravating nature and he loved to talk.

"Where were y'all at?" Jim said. "We got here last night and bedded down. Brenda said she thought you'd be back today, so we've just been hanging out. I always loved this place."

"Ella drug me and Caleb off to Hot Springs," Elijah answered. "It was supposed to be for a few hours, but we ended up staying the night."

About that time, Caleb walked in, "Tell him where we stayed pop. Tell him."

"We stayed at the Arlington," Elijah said, then pointing to Caleb. "And Scaredy cat here, was petrified. We practically had to drag him down the hall to our room."

Jimmy's eyes got big, "Eli, he's not far from right. There's lots of stories. Me and Brenda stayed once. I'll be honest. I don't really care to go back, but it is an interesting place. Maybe I need to have a little more faith, huh."

"Faith...what does that help anyway?" Elijah said in a derogatory manner, walking away, leaving Jimmy there just shaking his head. "I'll be in the living room."

Elijah got up to visit his sisters and could remember when they were just kids. When people think of identical twins, they were just that. You couldn't tell them apart except for one mark on the back of Brenda's neck. Other than that, it was impossible. Brenda told Elijah once, they switched places in class at school, and no one was the wiser. They got a good lashing for it, but no one really knew if they did it again or not. If they did, they didn't get caught.

"Hey brother," Brenda said, getting up and hugging his neck. "We're glad you came to visit us."

Laughing at her, Bridget added, "Make yourself at home."

"Very funny," he said. "I should call the law on you for trespassing."

"Call'em Eli," Jimmy said, his comical side glaring as always. "I know all the law around here...remember. I used to run into them all the time."

After that, Jimmy started telling tales from years ago, as well as everyone else, and laughter filled that room like it used to. His stories were too farfetched for fiction, but no one was sure if they were true or not. Regardless, they were quite entertaining, and his energy lifted everyone.

"How are you doing brother?" Brenda asked, resting her hand on his shoulder.

"I'm fine Brenda," he answered quickly. "Just fine."

Bridget started chuckling, "I remember when you met Geneva brother. You were up in the clouds, head over heels, in love from the minute go," she said. "Remember when you left us that one night to take a walk? You didn't know it, but we got up and followed you. We saw you sitting by a bush with her. After that, you were never the same."

"You followed me?" Elijah remarked. "But you told the folks I left you alone."

"Technically you did, but you know we were nosy little girls," Brenda finished.

Ella sat and listened to them and took it all in. From one story to the next, she loved hearing them all, whether they were true or not. It was her family and stories she could carry on. Leaning back on Caleb, his arm around her, neither said a word, only spectators to a show better than anything they could find on television.

After a while, Elijah loosened up and looked like he was enjoying himself. Between the, off the wall, unbelievable stories Jimmy told and stories from years past, the day flew by. Before they knew it, the sun was hiding for the night. Brenda, Bridget, and Ella made their way to the kitchen to whip up something for supper before everyone was too tired to eat, while the guys stayed in the living room continuing their conversation.

"I have a simple idea," Ella said. "Let's run to the store and get stuff to make burgers. I don't have it in me to do a big meal. Besides, the guys can grill, and it'll get us off the hook."

The girls agreed and did just that. It didn't take long to take the short drive to the nearest store, and when they made it back, Jimmy, Tom, and Caleb fired up the grill outback. They got supper fixed in a hurry. Before they knew it, the burgers were gone. It seemed like a pack of hungry wolves devoured them soon as they were ready. A few inhaled more than one but there was plenty to go around.

The moon flew high in the sky…doing its best to hypnotize them to sleep for the night after their bellies were full. Caleb laid back on the couch, eyes half-closed, and Ella rested her head on his chest with her arm wrapped around his waist.

"This is a lively group," Jimmy said, waltzing in the room after grabbing the last few fries left in the pan, his mouth full while he talked.

"It's been a long day Uncle Jimmy," Ella said, forcing a smile, her exhaustion from the day showing clearly through her tired eyes.

"At least there aren't any ghosts here, huh Caleb," Jimmy continued, letting out an unmistakable laugh they would know anywhere.

Caleb didn't even have the energy to respond to Jimmy's aggravating sense of humor, even though he wanted to. It was all he could do to stay awake long enough to crawl into bed.

Finally, everyone said goodnight and went to their rooms. One good thing, there were enough bedrooms in the house to accommodate, and Elijah made his way up the stairs. After such a tiring two days, his bones creaked with each step up, along with the boards under his feet. His body started to ache from the non-stop activity of the day and the car ride. *I'm not as young as I used to be*, he thought to himself.

He shut the door behind him and slowly make his way to the bed, then sat down with a long *Ahhh*. Elijah looked around at many memories around the room, and he got up to look at everything. From pictures to things Geneva had knitted and everything in between, in a way, it overloaded his brain with inundations of years past, years he desperately wanted back. He could faintly hear voices from the other rooms, but not enough to bother and he went back to the bed.

Elijah loved being with the family, but at the same time, welcomed the silence of the room, with only a few sounds of tree branches brushing up against the picture window. There was something about being alone. It forced him to face his thoughts, regrets, fears, and sorrows all by himself. Then, he opened the nightstand drawer and lifted out the envelope he found before Ella had the idea to go on a road trip. Slowly opening the dust-covered piece of paper enclosing a mystery his curiosity mulled over for two days since he found it.

Here goes, he muttered to himself, lifting it and opening the page.

CHAPTER EIGHT

Before his eyes, wasn't a letter exactly. It was a poem. There wasn't a date on it so he would know when it was written, but it did have Geneva's name at the bottom. She always loved to write, but he never paid much attention to her likes or wants after the newness of their relationship wore off. After a while, he did what he wanted and got more and more bitter as the years passed. That's the one thing he felt eating away at him every day.

Putting on his glasses, Elijah sat back up against a pillow and began to read the buried treasure of words.

LOOK TO HEAVEN

By Geneva James

I sit and look to Heaven
And pray my God above,
Will lead me in the right way
To guide the man, I love.
I close my eyes and wonder,
Can my faith transport to him?
But at the end of every night
The answer's looking grim.
So, I'll keep my eyes on Heaven
I'll raise my hand in praise.
Knowing when I'm gone from here
With the Lord, I'll spend my days.
Until then I'll give my worries,

> *My sadness and my grief,*
> *To my dear God in Heaven*
> *For he is my relief.*
> *I sit and look to Heaven*
> *Still praying to God above,*
> *That this man who has my heart,*
> *One day will know your love.*

Elijah lowered his hands, resting the paper on his lap. He could feel a rush of unbridled emotion take over like he never felt before. He laid down, halfway burying his head in the pillow, weeping. He didn't want anyone to hear him, but he couldn't hold it in. Her words rang loudly deep in his heart and soul, touching places he didn't know he had. The passion she felt spilled out into every line and entered him when he read it.

All these years, he said to himself. *All these years I didn't hear her. I didn't pay attention to what she was trying to tell me. Why find it now? Why now?*

Elijah folded the page and put it back where he found it, and his mind ran through every scenario, every time he was less than kind to her. Even when she was being good to him, whatever wall he put up, stayed between them. But he had to think of good times, or everything would eat him alive.

He turned off the light and climbed under the covers, the pages of time in his memory searching for something, anything to put a smile on his face, if only for a moment. The more he thought, the more tired he became. He didn't pick a moment in time, the sandman chose it for him, lifting him out of his body and placing him somewhere else.

*

"My lands," Geneva said, driving up to the big white house at the end of the dirt road off the highway. "Would you look at that? Looks like a small plantation house, don't it honey? Oh, my gracious."

"Needs a little fixin' up Geneva," Elijah said.

"I know," she replied demandingly. "Its home is what I think. You look at them hills out there. Oh, by golly what a view. It's like Heaven on earth."

"What does Heaven look like Geneva?" Elijah said, hints of arrogance showing. "Tell me."

"I can tell ya this much Elijah. The way you're a goin' you won't ever find out. But you better betcha I gotta mansion up there just like this one," she responded in her spunky, straightforward manner as usual.

"Mansion like this?" he smirked. "I guess you'll be fixing it up there too."

Taking her fist and hitting him in the arm as hard as she could, "Elijah James…I love you, but you work on my nerves. I don't know why I stay with you."

Elijah realized his attitude went a little too far, "I'm sorry Geneva. I truly am. Sometimes I don't know what gets into me."

"I can tell ya," she responded quickly, giving a quick nod. "It's the ole devil. I don't let'em have me and I wish you'd fight him off more than ya do."

They pulled up to the house, got out and walked around the place. The inspiring wrap around porch was stunning, but needed a little tender loving care, as did the flower beds around the front. The paint, a hint cracking, but to Geneva, all fixable. She knew she was due to have their baby in a few short months, and if they wanted it, action needed to be taken right away. Elijah made a pretty good chunk of money working on the pipeline for a while, enough for a down payment, and then some.

They found the key the realtor left for them to go in and check out, and Geneva was awestruck from the first step inside. The stairway with the beautiful railings curving up and around gave an elegant look, and the living room with the wood-burning stove in the corner, kept it rustic. As she made her way into the kitchen, simplicity could describe it best, but Geneva *was* simple, so it was perfect.

"Oh Elijah, this place makes me feel...uh, I just can't explain it. It's like we were supposed to find it. You know what I mean?" she said, letting her gorgeous smile decorate the room.

"Maybe so," he said, also seeing what an incredible place it could be with a few touches here and there.

"Maybe?" she said, raising her voice. "You've lost your blame mind if you don't make this our home. You hear me, Elijah?"

Elijah, with no other choice, gave in to her one-of-a-kind attitude and the giddy look on her face. He knew she wanted it, so without another word spoken, "Let's go see how long it'll take to get this place," Elijah smiled, letting the wall come down for a moment, knowing she needed it. "We can afford it and I guess you're..."

"I'm what," her hands landing on her hips, boldness rearing its ugly head once more.

"You're worth it," grinning, surprising her with kind words instead of his usual short snippy ones.

"Why looky there," she said, letting a short cackle, "You can be sweet." Then looking above. "See there Lord, there is hope."

Elijah rolled his eyes at her, and not having a response to her remarks, he took her hand and led her back to the car. Since it was the beginning of fall, those fallen leaves whipped around them as the cooling breeze caressed their faces. Geneva kept looking back to the house, excitement oozing out of her.

Suddenly, his mind flashed forward. Elijah was at the hospital, waiting for the doctor to come out, his nerves shook him from head to toe. People kept coming and going, but he hadn't seen hide nor hair of the doctor. Then, the door by the nurse's station flew open. Up walked a tall, broad fellow with greying hair.

He extended his hand to Elijah," I'm Dr. Holder and I'm proud to say you have a beautiful and healthy baby girl."

"I have a daughter?" Elijah said, sitting down to process it. "I'm really a dad."

"Geneva's a little groggy, but you can come back if you like," the doctor motioned.

Elijah jumped up and followed him with a smile like he'd never worn before. But then again, he never had a daughter before. As they reached her room, he took a deep breath and went inside.

Geneva was lying there looking exhausted and beautiful at the same time, holding the tiniest little thing. Going over, Elijah kissed Geneva and the baby on the forehead and stared at them.

"My girls," he whispered, finding emotions new to him.

"She's beautiful ain't she?" Geneva said, cradling her little girl, making sure no one took her away.

"Just like her mama," Elijah said, right on cue, wishing the moment would last forever.

"I don't have a name for her yet honey," Geneva muttered. "We have to think of the perfect name."

Elijah thought hard but couldn't come up with anything. His focus couldn't shy away from the vision in front of him. Besides, he never was much of a thinker. Geneva carried all the creative ideas and things, but he tried.

"How about Ella?" she said, her eyes lighting up. "Ella Rose."

"Ella Rose it is Geneva," he replied, eyes smiling back at her. "It's the perfect name for our little girl."

"Ella," Elijah heard someone call out from down the hallway.

"Is breakfast ready," Jimmy's voice rang loud and clear. "I want biscuits and gravy."

Elijah hit the bed with his fists and laid there, eyes opened once more by something taking him away from his memories, his dreams. *Dad blame Jimmy,* Elijah said to himself, whipping the covers off and throwing on some pants to go downstairs and entertain the house full of people who invited themselves.

Elijah held onto the railing, going down the stairs, being careful. That house was great when they were younger, but at times, those stairs were a little more taxing as years were added. They used to be able to run up and down them like it was nothing, but after a long while, running wasn't an option any longer.

"Good morning dad," Ella greeted, standing at the stove. "How you want your eggs?"

"Ummm," in a sleepy tone. "Scrambled I suppose."

"Same for me," Caleb rang in, already dressed and making his way to sit at the table. "Morning pop."

Still trying to completely wake up from the inspiring bits of his memories coming to life, Elijah simply nodded. Elijah never was a morning person. Then the entire crew came in, knowing there wasn't enough room at the four-chair table.

"Why don't we eat on the porch?" Ella said, getting everyone's plates all fixed up in a hurry. Agreeing, they all put on a light jacket and started outside, finding a spot at the several tables and chairs on the left, long side of the porch.

The wind was blocked to a degree, by the house, and the view of the hills in the distance was picturesque. Jimmy aggravated Brenda constantly, as usual, but Tom wasn't that way. His very reserved nature was calming and kind, along with Bridget's. They made the perfect pair. Ella and Caleb, on the other hand, didn't have much to say. Like the night before, they enjoyed sitting back and listening to the stories. Not a silent moment was had on the porch during breakfast. Where one would leave off, another would pick up and so on. It helped Elijah to keep his mind off things bothering him.

"What's today's plan?" Jimmy asked, cleaning his plate, and gulping down the last of his morning coffee.

"I've had a very eventful last few days," Elijah replied. "All of you go and do something. I might just sit here and rest."

"Mama always said if you lose your gitty up and go, it's gone," Ella smiled, laughing after. "So, what do you say dad?"

"I think my gitty up has gone," he replied with a chuckle.

"Nonsense brother," Brenda spoke up. "Let's go downtown. There's supposed to be a festival going on today on Broad Street with all kinds of music and food. It's been a long time since I went to one of those things."

"Me too," Bridget added. "We won't take no for an answer."

Being roped into going somewhere, once more, Elijah let out a big sign, "I guess I'm outvoted."

"Yes," everyone said in unison, finding humor in it.

What am I going to do with this family, he thought to himself? Then he realized it was much better than being there alone, so he embraced the invite and played follow the leader.

"Hey," Brenda said. "I think they have karaoke too. Jimmy might get up and sing for us."

"Might…if they're singing, I'll get up there. I'll show 'em how it's done." Jimmy grinned. "They'll think Garth Brooks was in the building."

Elijah remembered what good times he used to have at the many festivals downtown over the years, and the idea to go was perfect timing. Texarkana wasn't a huge town, but big enough, and enjoying things like that, could only add to the new memories he needed to make to continue forward, instead of always looking back. All looking back did, was make him face things he was sorry for. So, it was time to start making new memories that held positive value.

"We'll get these dishes done in a hurry and you guys start getting ready," Ella said, her, Brenda, and Bridget, gathering everyone's plates. "Two bathrooms only go so far at one time, you know."

"Waiting on three women to get ready…oh geeze. We won't get there until tonight," Jimmy blurted out, his one-of-a-kind laugh sneaking out.

"I'll take extra-long since you said that," Brenda said, giving a grin and a wink.

Elijah sat and listened to that crazy bunch he called *family*, shaking his head, wondering if everyone had such interesting kin folk. One thing was true, they sure brought color to his life. Without them, he would be wandering around in those halls and outside, alone, looking for something to bring a smile to his face. As it stood, he had a group of, so called, *comedians*, always finding a way to make him and everyone else find humor in everyday life.

"Remember what mama always said dad?" Ella asked, not really wanting him to answer, but made him think about it just the same.

"*You gotta laugh, honey*," Geneva would say. "*If you don't, you'll die with a frown on your face. And God don't like no frowns.*"

Elijah figured he would enjoy the company while he had it. Soon enough they would all be gone, living their own lives, and leaving that place with a ghost town feel to it. One thing Elijah didn't want to be, was alone.

Everyone got ready one at a time. All the while, Jimmy aggravated everyone he could, especially Brenda. It was a trademark of his. Everyone used to say if he ever stopped annoying people, something was wrong with him. Something about him, drew folks in. His sight was bad, and one eye was completely blind, but no one would ever know it. The positive attitude he carried around, overshadowed anything negative he was going through. For that, Elijah admired Jim and enjoyed his wit.

It took a while, but all seven got dressed without much of a hitch and they loaded into two cars, headed downtown. Following the foursome to town, Caleb started talking about the town and its history, asking questions. He knew some things but living it had much more vividness than reading about it in a history book. Elijah lived it. He watched it grow from one strip of a town where everyone gathered to the town it finally became.

"Downtown Texarkana used to be the happening place son," Elijah said. "People were everywhere. Businesses were booming. In fact, that's where everything took place because the rest of the city was rural. Until everything expanded and the mall came in years later, it was the cat's meow. I swear so many people gathered there, it was shoulder to shoulder and cars as far as you could see."

"That's where you met Geneva, huh Pop?" he continued his questioning, already knowing the story, but wanting to keep Elijah talking.

"It was son. It was," Elijah replied, remembering like it was yesterday. "She was a sight, but feisty from the minute go."

Caleb turned off highway 82 after going under the bridge and started seeing cars going in the same direction. That end of Broad St. seemed a hair abandon, but the further down, it picked up. When they approached the event site, folks were crawling everywhere. Young and old, there were people roaming the sidewalks and the festival area.

"There's tons of folks out today," Ella squealed as Caleb pulled up to park on fourth and Broad. "This will be such fun."

"Not for my wallet," Caleb remarked, knowing Ella would have a good time buying anything and everything.

Ella just gave him a look and that's all it took. Caleb didn't utter another as they got out of the car. Families passed by, holding the hands of their kids, while smiles were painted across their faces. The music rang loud and clear, and everyone couldn't help but move to the beat. From a distance, they could see cotton candy vendors, hot dogs, burgers, funnel cakes, games, and more.

Jimmy parked and they all followed the crowd, sticking together. There were vendors selling jewelry and handmade nick-knacks, candles, and lots more. It was right up Ella's alley. She would begin to twitch at the thought of shopping in any sense, so she was in hog heaven. Of course, Brenda and Bridget were the same. They loved shiny things, fake or real. They were always that way, and those three made a beeline to the first jewelry place they saw. They picked up everything, seeing how it would look on them, and chatting with each other the entire time.

"Oh boy," Caleb said. "Here we go again Pop."

Jimmy and Tom looked at each other, shrugged their shoulders, and waited. There was nothing else they could do. You could tell they learned through the years what makes a marriage work. They learned that letting the women have her way, most of the time, was part of it. So, patience got embedded into them. It was the kind of patience a man had to have.

Elijah looked up and noticed a Ferris wheel on the far left, but a little smaller than at a big fair. People were lined up to ride it, including kids. It brought back fond memories, the kind that never left the depths of his mind. Walking off from Jimmy, Tom, and Caleb, he went toward it, slowly losing present time to the past holding him captive.

CHAPTER NINE

E lijah and Geneva were holding Ella's hand, only six years old at the time, walking to the Ferris wheel at the annual four states fair one fall evening. The sounds of the fair were unmistakable, from bells ringing, music playing, and carnies calling folks over to their booth. From games to rides, there was something to do everywhere you looked. Ella loved all the lights and her eyes lit up with excitement and joy created springs in her feet, bouncing up and down.

"Can we ride it, daddy?" Ella asked sweetly, her begging eyes looking up at him. "Please."

"Ella," Elijah replied, a little fear in his eyes. "Daddy doesn't like heights. You and your mama can ride. I'll just watch."

"Come on honey, it ain't that high," Geneva added, flashing her brilliant blue eyes at him, and batting those long eyelashes. "Now how can you say *no* to that face?"

Elijah glanced down at Ella. She was still peering at him, never changing her expression. Ella always knew how to get to him from the time she was born. Even when he wanted to say no, somehow, he never stuck with it. She was the

"Ok, I will," he said, shaking in his voice. "But don't let me fall."

"Oh daddy," Ella said, dragging him the remainder of the way to the ride, thinking he was trying to be funny. "We won't fall."

Geneva couldn't help but give her normal laugh, treading behind them. She knew Elijah didn't like anything about being high up in the least. He would barely climb a normal ladder, but for Ella, he would.

"Room for two more," the carney said, pointing at them. "Three more I guess, with your little one in the middle. Get in and lock your bar."

"Lock my bar?" Elijah muttered. "They need to make sure it's locked?"

Geneva, hearing Elijah talking to himself, put her arm around Ella and squeezed him on the arm, "It's not like we're goin' that far up. Don't you scare our girl. Goodness, gracious, God ain't gonna let nothin' happen to us."

"Maybe not you, but…" Elijah started to say when the ride took off.

From that moment, Elijah closed his eyes, feeling the car they were in, begin to go up further and further. Everything in him dropped to the pit of his stomach then back again as it would drop down and repeat over and over. It continued for several minutes then stopped them at the very top, letting people off at the bottom.

"Why are they leaving us up here," Elijah said, panic prominent in his voice.

"If I still had my ole trusty cross," Geneva said. "I'd give it to ya. It always protected me."

What she said, took his mind off the ride momentarily, "What happened to it? I guess you never mentioned that. I always thought you still had it."

"Wish I knew," she answered. "I had it one day and the next, it was gone. I figured I laid it down somewhere and just forgot where. I looked and looked, but there was no use."

"I'll have to get you a new cross," he said, feeling a little relief since they were making their way down to solid ground.

"Na," she grinned. "It was special. Besides, God's with me whether I have that with me or not. He's my cross."

"Maybe I'll understand one day Geneva," he said, finally stopping, being let out of, what he considered to be a death trap.

"You will honey. I promise you will," she said with a quick peck on the cheek.

"Can I have a cross mama," Ella asked sweetly.

"You betcha you can honey," Geneva said, kneeling to Ella's level, looking proud she asked such a thing at her age. The look of thankfulness showed with a simple question from their daughter.

They went to several different vendors, and one was a jewelry stop. One of the first things Ella saw, was a necklace with a small cross on it. In the center sat a tiny dot.

"What's that?" Ella asked, looking at the necklace ever so carefully.

Geneva picked it up and began to tell her the story, backing it up with scripture. "You see Ella, this is a mustard seed in the center of this cross. Do you know what that means?

"No mama," she said, but attentive showing she wanted to know.

Geneva knelt down once more, "We all need to have mustard seed faith. Jesus said faith small as a mustard seed can move mountains. Like it says in Matthew *"The kingdom of heaven is like a grain of mustard seed that a man took and sowed in his field. It is the smallest of all seeds, but when it has grown it is larger than all the garden plants and becomes a tree, so that the birds of the air come and make nests in its branches."*

"I'm little like that seed," Ella smiled, never taking her eyes off the cross for a moment. "And I'm going to grow big and strong."

"Yes, you are honey," Geneva said, hugging her, then standing up and looking at the woman behind the booth. "I'll take it. It's a little long, but she'll grow into it."

"Really mama…really?" Ella said, excitement dancing in her eyes.

Geneva paid the lady and then clasped it around Ella's neck, and something special happened then and there. It's like God created a bond between those two no one could ever break. It was a moment in time, no one could relive or recreate, but priceless instead. Like one moment in time that would live on, it was just that.

"Dad," a voice said from behind him.

Turning around, was the same Ella, but suddenly a grown woman instead. How fast the mind can make you travel back and forth, but looking at her, "Do you still have the necklace," Elijah asked, never really thinking about it until then.

Ella thought for a moment, "This one," she said, reaching around her neck and letting the small cross show, resting it on the outside of her shirt. "I always wear it dad."

"Do you remember that day?" he asked, seeing if her memory was just as vivid as his own.

Taking a moment of silence, "It was a day like today," she said. "I remember the ride and you being scared, then mama talking about her cross she lost."

"Yes," Elijah smiled sincerely.

"I remember," Ella continued. "Asking if I could have a cross like hers or something like that. I didn't really think she'd say yes, but…"

Elijah reached over and lifted the cross around her neck, "But she did, didn't she?"

"And I still remember the story of the mustard seed. I'll never forget it. It's in Matthew I believe. I have that kind of faith dad," Ella smiled, reaching for his hand. "Are we ready to catch up with the rest of the crew? They're about to drive me nuts. Oh, and I think I bought too much jewelry…not sure where I'll put it all."

Without a word, feeling grateful for the moment they had, they walked toward the others. You could hear Jimmy from a mile away. Elijah used to tell Jim he didn't need a microphone for people to hear him, his voice just carried. He had compelling ways to keep you tuned in to what he was saying, and his comedic dialog was never boring.

"We looked all over for you Pop," Caleb said, sitting at a picnic table eating one of the largest funnel cakes anyone ever saw. "You want some?"

"He was just walking around, checking things out," Ella said. "Actually, he figured if we all started acting crazy, he didn't want people to associate him with us."

Elijah couldn't help but laugh at Ella's explanation as to why he wandered off and followed along behind them. They ate so much junk food, it's a wonder none of them got sick. Crowds of people were everywhere reminding Elijah of the old days. Of course, back in those days, it was the only place to hang out, except being at home. And that's what the older folks did.

Several hours flew by like minutes, but the people continued sifting in. Elijah, always being used to a little nap mid-day, started to tire. No one else noticed, but Ella did. They always had a connection from the day she came into the world. Still, years later, that connection grew even stronger. There's something about a father-daughter relationship. Although unspoken, it's a powerful thing.

"Guys," Ella said. "I'm a little worn out. You ready to head home?"

"What?" Jimmy said. "You're the youngest of the bunch and you're tired."

"Me and dad can go on home and y'all can stay if you want," Ella said, linking arms with Elijah. "We don't want to ruin your fun."

"I'll hang with them for a while," Caleb said. "If that's okay with you."

Ella smiled and kissed Caleb on the cheek, "It's fine. Enjoy yourself. See you guys in a bit."

Ella and Elijah headed to the car, the faint breeze comforting them. It didn't seem like the crowd was thinning much and the music rang out in every direction. Elijah looked around and up and down Broad St., remembering the bustle of the past. To him, it was hard to believe things changed so much. From the way people dressed, to hairstyles and the way cars have evolved in a futuristic way.

"What are you thinking dad?" Ella asked, starting up the car.

With a slight chuckle, "My mind's been wandering a lot lately. I can't seem to control it. It's like I'm living in the past more than I am in the present."

"That's understandable, but at some point, we all have to face reality. Everything will be fine. We just have to believe," Ella stated sweetly.

"Just like your mama," he said. "That faith talk and all."

"It's not just talk dad. It's truth," Ella explained.

"I don't' know what's true or false these days," he replied, sadness in his tone.

Ella tried to figure out how to get him to find something optimistic to think about. She thought and thought. And watching him sit there like a lost soul, trying to find a direction to go that didn't have a dead-end, was torture for her.

"Tell me something about mama that makes you happy dad...a memory you treasure. I know you got plenty," Ella said.

Thinking for a minute about what she asked, he started to laugh like someone just told the funniest joke. He shook his head and looked at Ella. "I remember one time," he said, laughing still. "Your mama was in the kitchen fixing breakfast. You know how much she loved making those home-made biscuits of hers. She always said her grandma taught her and I never doubted it."

"She made the best," Ella said, listening for more.

"Anyway," he continued. "I was set to head back out of town on the pipeline for a month, considering we had a place to pay for. Geneva had just pulled a hot pan of biscuits out of the oven and buttered them all with that old-time real butter."

"Where was I," Ella asked.

"You were at school," he said. "But she wanted to make me something to eat before I went off to work."

"What happened?" Ella asked.

"Well, she had to go upstairs for something and when she did, I went and ate one biscuit, then two…then,"

"No, you didn't," Ella chuckled, obviously entertained by his story.

"I ate every single one of them. It's like they melted right in my mouth, like butter. And man, they were good. But when she came down and saw they were gone, not leaving one for her, she was mad as hornet's nest."

"Dog gone you Elijah James," she said, slamming the pan down, her eyes turning red and giving a look that said more than words ever could.

"You get outa here right now," she said, slamming down the empty pan. *"I don't care if it is gonna be a month 'til you come home, you're just plain selfish. Just plain ole selfish."*

"What did you do?" Ella inquired.

"What do you think I did," Elijah laughed. "I left. She started throwing things at me like she was having target practice and I figured it might take the entire month for her to stop being mad."

"I never heard you tell that sorry before," Ella said, shaking her head in disbelief and laughing.

"It's because if I ever brought it up again, she would've gotten mad all over again," Elijah said, giving a genuine smile. "By the way Ella, why is it that women get mad again for something that's already happened. Does it ever go away? It sure didn't with your mama."

"Ask Caleb," Ella winked. "He'll probably tell you no, but sometimes I just act like I'm mad to get my way. I guess it's just a woman for ya dad."

They enjoyed their peaceful drive, just the two of them, talking and reminiscing. Ella turned down the road toward the house. Dust danced all around the car, spitting rocks left and right to the side, then cleared while pulling up the drive.

Parked to the right of the porch, was Sheriff Talley, standing there leaning against her car. She had been sheriff in those parts for several years and did just as good or better a job than any man could. With her, was Terry Robertson, her trusty side kick deputy, always doing whatever he was told to do.

Elijah got out of the car, curious what would bring her to his house, and he slowly walked her direction, his mind doing cartwheels before a word was even spoken.

"Sheriff," Elijah nodded cordially. "What do we owe the pleasure of your visit?"

CHAPTER TEN

"I'm not really sure how to start," sheriff Talley said.

"Just say it," Elijah replied, letting his imagination run away with him before she could say another word.

"I don't really know if this is good news or bad news Elijah, but we found Geneva's car," she said.

Terry added, "The police found it abandon in Baton Rouge, Louisiana a few days back, but just now got us the information we needed to confirm it was hers."

I thought she left me; Elijah muttered to himself. *I was sure she left me.*

Ella started to cry, "So you think she's...she's..."

"We're not saying anything Ella," Sheriff Tally said, putting her hand on Ella's shoulder. "All we know is her car was in Baton Rouge, but it's being brought here. We don't know where she is."

"What can we do? Where can we go? Where do we look?" Ella said hysterically.

"Calm down," Terry said, kindly intervening. "Let us get the car and see if there are any clues and go from there. We are on it, I promise."

Ella hugged Terry for his compassion for the situation, then turned to Elijah, her eyes full of tears. "Dad, maybe she's..."

"I don't want to think about it," Elijah replied, almost in an angry manner. "Everyone kept saying she'd be back, and hope has killed my soul. Hope has made me lose sleep at night thinking everything would be just fine. Hope has taken the place of the healing I needed. It kept me thinking one day she'd walk back through that door, but I know the truth. She's never coming back. She's gone and it's not okay."

Elijah didn't say another word, but instead, at a faster pace than usual, went to the house and slammed the front door. If it wasn't for the sounds of nature around as always, silence would have prevailed. Sheriff Tally didn't know what to say, knowing the hurt Elijah had gone through since the day Geneva left. And Terry, such a big-hearted guy, wanted to find words of comfort, but none could be found.

"Please let us know if you have any more information," Ella smiled. "Thank you for coming out and...I'll take care of dad. He's just..."

"We understand," the sheriff smiled. "We all miss her."

"Shoot," Terry added. "She had more energy than anyone half her age and a firecracker to say the very least."

"I'll pray about it," Ella said softly. "If there's anything I've learned from my mama, it's to pray. She always said that God won't put more on us than we can handle, but right now, he's pushing the envelope a bit."

"How about we pray with you," Nancy said, her and Terry going over to Ella, all holding hands. *"Dear Lord in Heaven. We need you today. This family needs you today. We know you know miss Geneva well. We know you know where she is, whether it's with you or somewhere else, but please keep her safe either way. God if she's not with you, help us find our way to her. She has touched every life she's ever crossed, and we want to give back to her by not giving up. Give us strength and guide us in the right direction. We ask all of this in Jesus' name...AMEN"*

Tears found their way down all their faces with the power of prayer. No more words needed to be spoken. Leaving it with prayer was how Geneva would want it. Sheriff Talley and Terry got in the car and drove away slowly.

Ella followed in her dad's path to the house, and her heart was sinking at the possibility her mother was really gone. So many things could've happened, but there was no sense in trying to sort anything out until there was enough information to go on. It would only make things worse to try. Elijah, on the other hand, was tired of holding out hope, and with the new information, he looked completely hollow inside.

Ella went upstairs and quietly stepped toward Elijah's room. Not a sound other than the few of the creaking planks as she walked.

"Dad," whispered Ella, opening his cracked bedroom door.

"Go away," Elijah said, sitting on his bed staring toward the window.

"But..."

"It's all my fault!" he yelled, not necessarily directed to Ella, but a statement instead. "I should've..."

"What are you talking about dad?" Ella asked, confused, and going over and sitting on the small vanity stool by the dresser. "What's your fault?"

"She wanted me to..." Elijah started to say, when...

"I'm home," a loud voice rang out, Jimmy's to be exact, as they could hear the front door open and shut. Heavy footsteps headed up the stairs in their direction, and Jim poked his head around the doorway.

"We would've stayed longer," he said. "But they started playing that kind of music you can't even understand what they're saying, and that was it. Give me country or Gospel any day to that mess."

The look on Elijah's and Ella's faces said enough. He knew he had interrupted something but wasn't sure exactly what. No one said anything for a moment, then Elijah got up and pushed past Jimmy, then downstairs.

"What's up with him," Jimmy said, shrugging his shoulders like he said something wrong.

"Uncle Jimmy," Ella murmured, doing the same as her dad, finding her way to the rest of the family who knew nothing about their recent findings about her mom.

She didn't know exactly how to bring it up or even if she should. Her main concern, her dad, and how he was handling the news. For the moment, her own thoughts and feelings fell by the waist side to care for him. Nothing seemed more important.

Ella went outside and sat on the swing by herself. She reflected on a time etched in her memory. It transcended space and time, just like it happened yesterday. She closed her eyes, and her heart and mind took her back to a special moment.

Geneva and Ella were sitting on that very swing one hot summer day, in their usual spots. Their talks were always the best and always meaningful. It's like Geneva always knew exactly what to say to make everyone smile, and her genuineness spilled out with every word she spoke.

"Ella honey," Geneva said. "I'm so darn proud a you. I don't tell you enough, but God did me right when he made you, my daughter."

"Thank you, mama," Ella smiled and grasped her hand. "I think I'm pretty lucky too. You were supposed to be mine."

"You know what," Geneva continued. "When I was in that there hospital, bringin' you into this world, I prayed the entire time. I prayed through hurt and pain. I knew that pain would bring a miracle into this world. I prayed God would help me lead you to him one day. Nobody knows what's in other folk's heart, but I think I know where your heart is honey. I see it in your eyes. I see it in your actions and how you treat people."

"You did lead me mama," Ella replied sincerely, still holding her hand. "I know him."

"Oh, baby," Geneva said, her tears starting to trickle down, full of joy. "You don't know how happy that makes me. I'd be terrified if I thought about being in my big ole mansion up there without you."

"I'll be there mama. I promise."

"I don't know about your dad though. Sometimes I think God has been a testin' me for more years than I can count, to see how long I can be an example for that bitter old man. But I won't give up. That's where faith comes in honey. If I told you that once, I told you a hundred times. You gotta have faith. Without it, ain't nothin' possible."

Both feeling the crosses engraved on each side of the swing, as they always did, they got up to go inside.

"Mama," Ella stopped, turning Geneva to her. "Thank you for being my mama. I don't know what I would've done without you."

Geneva had no words, but more tears instead. There was something about her, letting emotions take control and the waterworks would flow freely. Their embrace was more than love, it was spiritual, confirming what Geneva thought she knew, filling her heart completely with peace.

Still swinging and coming back to the present time, Ella's thoughts left a smile on her face she didn't think could be wiped off. The vivid memories of her mom and the inspirational way she always put things, stayed present in Ella's heart and mind. In fact, those ways were what led her in life's path...a path to faith and believing in the unseen and an eternal future only through God.

Ella, looking toward the hills, whispered "Thank you, mama."

In the distance, dark clouds were congregating in several clusters, and the wind began to pick up almost instantly. The tall grass on one part of the property, swayed back and forth, like nature doing a dance for her. Not being one who liked storms, Ella went back inside, walking into a conversation Jimmy and Tom were having.

"Looks like a storm," Jimmy said, pulling the curtains back just enough to see.

"I hate storms," Ella remarked, going over and sitting next to Caleb.

"She does," Caleb laughed. "One night I had to go out of town and a huge storm blew through. She said she heard all kinds of scary noises and called everyone she knew to come stay with her.

"I did not," Ella responded quickly. "I only called one person. And you're a fine one to talk about being scared."

"Well," Elijah interrupted, his tone very poignant. "It'll pass. We've been through bad weather and this house is still standing."

"Hey Eli," Jimmy said. "We've got to leave tomorrow evening, but why don't we all go down to that Cowboy Church Geneva always went to. We went there a few times too. She a greeter there or something?

Everyone but Elijah gave a firm yes, but Elijah didn't say a word. He was always strange when anyone started talking about faith and God. He continued staring at the television that wasn't even turned up loud enough to hear what they were saying.

"Sound good Pop?" Caleb asked.

"I guess it won't kill me," Elijah answered, taking the remote and turning the volume up to tune them out.

"I don't have my bible with me," Ella said.

"Your mother's is on the buffet on the entry. I imagine you could use it," Elijah said, pointing in the appropriate direction.

"Thank you, Dad," Ella smiled. "It would be an honor."

It wasn't long and the trees started whipping around like a monsoon was coming and the whistling sound of the heavy wind rang out like it might blow the house clean away. Then came the rain. Like God had let the bottom out of the sky, it pounded down on the metal roof, leaving echoes of Heaven's tears, all around them.

"God must be angry tonight," Bridget said, cuddling close to Tom. "It's been a long time since I've seen this kind of rain."

What she said, reminded Elijah of something. Like it happened yesterday, it was clear in his mind.

"Remember when you two were kids," Elijah said, looking at Brenda and Bridget. "This horrendous thunderstorm came up suddenly. Before we all knew it, the tornado alarm in town started blowing loud."

"I do remember that?" Bridget asked. "I had almost forgotten."

"Mom and Dad weren't home, and we all thought we were going to get blown away, so we all hid in the bathroom and climbed in the tub."

"We did," Brenda added. "Then we heard something that sounded like a train."

Elijah, halfway laughing, "I swear that darn tornado went down the field, a few blocks in length over, but we could hear it like it was about to fly us away like Dorothy in the wizard of oz."

"Oh, my goodness brother," Bridget said. "We knew you were as scared as we were, but you wouldn't show it. You had to be the big bad big brother. You never wanted to show you were afraid of anything, but we knew."

Slightly grinning at his little sister, "I suppose I was a little scared."

About that time, a flash of lightning lit right next to the window, followed by a tremendous clash of thunder, shaking the entire room. Everyone jumped at the same time. The beautiful sky from earlier in the day had been swallowed up by darkness and black clouds filled with power rumbling the skies.

Elijah, knowing his sisters and brother in-laws would have to be leaving the following evening, figured it best to at least pretend everything was okay, even if it wasn't. So, he got up and started a fire, and went into the kitchen to fix hot chocolate for everyone. Elijah took his time and could hear the rest of them still swapping stories, mostly Jimmy, and the sounds in the house-made him smile inside.

In a few days, I'll be by myself again, Elijah thought to himself. *What will I do then?*

"Can I help Eli?" Jimmy asked, coming up behind him secretively.

Without a yes or no, he smiled and handed Jimmy a few cups of hot chocolate while Elijah put the rest on a tray and carried them. Careful not to fidget too much as to spill any, he set the tray down on the coffee table in front of the fireplace. Each cup was snatched up in an instant and Elijah grabbed the last one.

"Oh, Pop," Caleb said. "This sure hits the spot."

"Yes," the rest agreed at the same time, steadily stirring, and sipping until it was cool enough to drink.

"This was mama's favorite," Ella said before she even thought. "I mean…"

Elijah couldn't take it any longer. He knew they would all find out sooner or later, so sooner was the better choice.

"Sheriff Talley and her deputy Terry Robertson came by this evening. They were here when Ella and I got home," Elijah started. "They came to tell us…to tell us…"

Ella, knowing such a thing was difficult for her dad to say, stepped in, "They found mama's car in Baton Rouge Louisiana a few days back, but there was no sign of her. That's all they know right now."

"What would she be doing in Baton Rouge?" Brenda said, expressing a look of shock.

"They don't know if she was or…they don't know anything else. The car is supposed to be brought here in a day or two, then they'll see if they can find something to go on," Ella finished. "That's why dad and I have been a little distant. It's hard to think about. It's hard to wonder where she is with no idea where to start."

"I thought I ran her away," Elijah said sadly. "I did run her away with my anger and rude talk. I ran her away by not letting her know I loved her. And she was so…"

"Dad, you didn't do anything," Ella said, although she wasn't sure exactly what happened.

"You're right, I didn't. I didn't do anything," he said, his emotions taking over as a few tears started to show. "That was my problem. I never did anything right by her."

Then he remembered the day it happened like it was yesterday. Every detail, every word spoken, and every feeling, came rushing back to him all over again, and he told the story to the ones he loved most.

CHAPTER ELEVEN

"**E**lijah honey, take me into town. I need to grab a few groceries and maybe go to a few stores and shop a little. By golly, I feel like I ain't been outa this house in ages," Geneva said, scurrying around as always, finishing up the few dishes from breakfast. "I swear these walls are closin' in on me. And you know how I like to go go go."

Elijah was Heading outside to work on a project he had started in the shop on the side of the house, and he turned to her with attitude. "I'm not going to town to shop Geneva; we'll go another time. I'm busy today."

"But you know I've been a little off lately honey. Like my memory is comin' and a goin'. And I don't want it to go if I'm out and about. We won't be long," she asked once more. "Come on sugar, it'll be fun."

Elijah raised his voice for no good reason at all, other than to be just plain mean, "I said no. We'll go another day. Didn't you hear me?"

Instantly, the kind, sweet look normally painted across her beautiful face, turned to something different. Her ice-blue eyes began to squint, and she made fists, planting them on her hips firmly. A smile was nowhere in sight, and she looked like she was ready to fight.

"I heard ya," she said in a snappy tone. "I heard ya Elijah. Gods got a lot a work to do on you, I swear. It's gonna take an overhaul once he gets started. And oh, I wish he'd go ahead and start."

"God?" Elijah remarked sarcastically, "I told you a long time ago, God don't know me and today's no different."

Geneva grabbed her bible, pen, and a notepad from the buffet in the entryway, and went into the living room, sitting down, her back to Elijah. She opened the bible to a specific page, knowing exactly what she was looking for. Then she put pen to paper and began to write. It's like her mind was turning and those words flowed out of her like a river flowing rapid.

"What are you doing?" Elijah asked her, his tone still rough and hurtful. "What are you writing?"

"None a your business," she snapped. "B'sides, you don't care about me or anyone else the way you're a actin. That ole devils got you Elijah and if you don't start seein' that, you're in more trouble than you'll ever know. You're mean as an ole' buzzard just like my grandfather was. You wasn't always like this, but you are now. I ain't a sure what happened to you, but I ain't standin' for it any longer."

"I'm not mean, just busy Geneva," he said, trying to calm her, using a hint kinder tone.

"Piddlin', busy piddlin'," she said, turning, one eye staring him down like she could kill him. "That's always more important than me, ain't it Elijah? Everything is more important than me. All I wanted to do was go to town. And I will by golly. I don't need you. I don't need you at all."

Elijah let out a huge breath in aggravation, "I'll be in the shop," he said, dismissing her verbal threats, and going on about his business. He was thinking the entire time, he was making a huge mistake, but ignoring those thoughts as quickly they arrived.

Elijah walked out of the house, but something told him to turn around an apologize. He had no reason for his quick temper taking over, no reason at all. But the stubborn side of him, kicked in as it always did and he didn't even hesitate, just went on his way.

It was more than ten or fifteen minutes and Elijah could hear a door slam and the car startup. *"What in the world,"* he said to himself, hurrying toward the sound.

"Geneva," he yelled loud as he could. "I'll take you. Stop!"

Before he knew it, a cloud of dust from their road, filled the air to where he could barely see down it. Suddenly she was gone. For whatever reason, Elijah didn't go after her, thinking she'd be back in a few hours, calmed down enough to fix up a nice supper. No other thoughts entered his mind, and he went back and finished what he started.

"Dad," Ella said, touching his shoulder. "It's okay?"

"I should've taken her...I should've taken her," Elijah began to weep. "Why didn't I just take her like she asked me to Ella? Why?"

For the first time since everyone got to the house, silence took over, everyone feeling Elijah's pain and the air around them was thick with hurt and regret, Elijah's. Caleb wasn't cracking funny jokes and Jimmy had no tales to tell. They just gathered around Elijah and gave what he needed the most in that moment, love, and comfort.

Getting all his feelings out in the open for the first time ever, something in him begin to change. Finally admitting to what he terribly regretted worked on him from the inside out.

"You couldn't have known Pop," Caleb said, looking at him with those caring eyes he always wore around. "There's no way you could've known."

"All this time I thought she left me because of how terrible I was to her, but now I know something might have happened to her because I was too busy." Elijah said desperately. "How could I be like that to the sweetest, most loving woman I've ever known? I have no excuse."

"Did you say she was writing something dad," Ella asked?

"Yes," Elijah answered. "Why?"

Ella went to the buffet, and there sat Geneva's bible just where Elijah said it would be. She picked it up and brought it back and sat down. She stared at the large, faded cover with binding that appeared to be very worn, almost trying to come apart, and rested it in her lap.

"Now let's see what you were writing mama," Ella whispered to herself, thumbing through those thin, gold-trimmed pages of her bible. About halfway through, some-thing stopped her. Opening to that page sat a piece of paper folded up.

"What is it?" Caleb asked, Elijah, looking on all the while.

Not replying to Caleb right away, unsure what it was herself, she opened the page. Immediately, she knew her mama's handwriting. It was unmistakable with all the loops and hoops she always used. She always said it made the words look fancy.

Ella began to read as everyone waited for her to tell them what it said. With eyes filled with tears, she lowered the newfound treasure and handed it over to Brenda. "You read it out loud," Ella said. "I can't."

Brenda did as her niece asked without any questions asked, and she started reading.

Dear God,

I know I've asked for your help more times than I want to count, but I need you now. That man I love is lost and that devils got his pitchfork clean into him and I can't seem to break through. God, I get so angry, and I know it's not right, but I just can't help it. He makes me so blame mad I can hardly stand it. I've been reading in your word, and it gives me comfort, but I wish it would give him comfort too. I wish he believed like I do. God, I don't want to go into eternity without him, but it looks like that's what's gonna happen. Please dear Lord watch over him and keep him safe. I don't ask anything for me. If he finds his way to you, that'll be gift enough.

AMEN

Ephesians 6: 10 – 11
James 4: 7
Romans 8: 37 – 39

Elijah sat there, hands covering his face very still. Brenda sat the page on the coffee table in the middle of them all. Elijah looked up, a hint of a light shining through is eyes, then he picked up the hidden note to God.

"What do these scriptures say?" he asked Ella. "I want to know. I need to know. It's like we were supposed to find this."

"Let me look dad," she said, still holding her mama's bible, then flipping through. "Ok, the first one is Ephesians chapter six verses ten and eleven, and it says *Finally, be strong in the Lord and in his mighty power. Put on the full armor of God, so that you can take your stand against the devil's schemes.*"

"Keep reading," Elijah asked, eyes closed, trying to absorb it all. "Please."

Once again, Ella found the next scripture her mama had made note of. It must've had significant meaning, or she wouldn't have written them down. Everything she did, was for a reason and most always, it was to please the creator.

"Okay, this is James chapter four, verse seven. *Submit yourselves, then, to God. Resist the devil, and he will flee from you.*"

"She thinks I'm the devil," Elijah said, sad eyes lingering, although he said it in a somewhat comical way. "I may be the devil."

"No, you're not dad," Ella said. "You're a good person, but we all get lost sometimes. Mama always taught me there's only one way. She taught me when I was little to pray, and that God will always be with me."

"I never did pray, not really," Elijah said, almost ashamed to say such a thing. "Geneva thought I was. I just acted like it to pacify her. Pretty sad huh."

"She was never going to give up on you," Bridget added. "She never gave up on anyone she set her sights on to lead to God."

"What's the last one she mentioned?" Elijah asked, wanting to hear the final scripture his beloved had on her mind before she left that day.

"The last one she mentioned, was Romans chapter eight, verses thirty-seven through thirty-nine," she said, trying to find it as swiftly as she could, not knowing the order of the books of the bible like she should. "Here we are…it says *No, in all these things we are more than conquerors through him who loved us. For I am convinced that neither death nor life, neither angels nor demons, neither the present nor the future, nor any powers, neither height nor depth, nor anything else in all creation, will be able to separate us from the love of God that is in Christ Jesus our Lord.*"

Elijah looked slightly confused. "I don't understand," he said, taking the bible from Ella's hands and skimming over those words hoping they would make sense.

"Pop," Caleb said, going over and sitting next to him. "It just means, if we believe and have faith in God and hang onto that faith for dear life, nothing can separate us from him. Truth be known, the one who usually separate us from God the most is ourselves."

"What do you mean?" Elijah listened intensely.

"So many times, we let everything else come before God. We treat those things as idols, worshiping our money, our careers, the want for fame…everything but worshiping him. And that's when your life falls apart when he's not a part of it," Caleb explained.

Without skipping a beat, Jimmy added, "He's right Eli. I was a mess a long time ago, but I didn't think I was. You remember how I was back in the day. It was nothing for me to cuss in every sentence, drink like it was going out of style, and partied all the time. I was just out for a good time. I made lots of money but didn't help people I should've. I just bought the most expensive of everything. I had it all wrong. I didn't know God and I wasn't happy either. I realized money don't make you happy."

"What about now?" Elijah asked curiously. "Are you happy now Jim?"

Jimmy looked at Brenda, and they both smiled, "I am happy. I put God first in my life and the puzzle pieces of my life finally fit. You see Eli, there's no sense in searching for answers when all you have to do is turn to Him. He has all the answers. I wish I'd known that when I was younger. But I guarantee you he saved my life a few times, more than I want to count. He saved me for a reason."

Elijah kept holding Geneva's bible close and started feeling things, unusual things. Instead of being mad, looking around him, he was grateful for his family. That crazy, unpredictable, and incredible bunch of folks who tried to complete what Geneva started, were guiding him in the right direction.

"Are we going to that cowboy church tomorrow," Elijah asked boldly, still clutching that old bible. "If so, I need to find something to wear."

"You come as you are," Caleb said. "That's their saying. They just want to share the good news with you."

"The good news?" Elijah asked, then laughed, knowing what he meant. "I got it."

"Glad to hear it Pop," Caleb replied, his infectious smile glaring at everyone in the room. "It'll be a great Sunday."

"You betcha," Ella said, trying to sound like her mama, and kind of did, making it even more authentic by the arms motion she did just like Geneva.

Elijah couldn't help but smile, almost hearing her voice as Ella said such a thing. And then, things got back to normal when Caleb noticed the time…supper time. Everyone could almost hear his stomach making conversation and the look on Caleb's face showed it.

"It's about time to…" Caleb started.

"Eat," Brenda and Bridget said in unison. "We'll get on it before you pass out."

"Thank you," he said. "I have to have my nourishment, ya know."

The rest of the evening flew by simply spending time together. Elijah had never enjoyed it more than he did that day. There was something different about it than before. There was no getting cranky and short with anyone or saying something offensive. It was just a special time. The girls whipped up supper in no time and they all found a place to sit and eat…the girls were in the kitchen and the guys in the living room watching something on television. Laughter filled the place in the most genuine manner, covering it with peace and joy.

The grandfather clock in the corner of the living room rang out. It was ten o'clock and they were all still *jibber-jabbering*, as Geneva would say, and it wasn't long before they retired to their rooms. Elijah and Ella were the last two.

"Dad, I'm proud of you," Ella said, giving him the sweetest peck on the cheek.

"Why Ella? I haven't done anything to make you proud," Elijah answered, still feeling ashamed.

"I'm just proud you're my dad, that's all," she said, giving a wink and going to their room.

Elijah stood there alone for a moment and the house finally got quiet, with only a little wind making music outside and he placed the bible where Ella got it from. He ran his callused hands over the antique looking cover, smiled and muttered, *Goodnight, Geneva*, hoping wherever she was, she could hear him.

To his room he went, a few squeaking boards beneath his feet on the way. Then, turning in for the night, tried his best to wind down. With only the light from the bedroom window, Elijah gave a long exhale.

"*Where are you, Geneva?*" he said to himself. Such a question reminded him of a similar time, but different, as his dreams whisked him away.

CHAPTER TWELVE

Elijah, coming back in town early to surprise Geneva after being away on a job for over three weeks, arrived with flowers in hand and her favorite chocolates. Geneva always loved the smell of fresh flowers in the house, and she had a sweet tooth that wouldn't quit. He knew she would love it and his romantic motion was magnified since he never had much of one to start with. He knew she would appreciate such a gesture, but when he pulled up to the house, there was no Geneva. It was midafternoon and he figured she just ran to town for groceries or something. But hours later she still wasn't home.

Finally, a few hours after dark, Geneva's headlights lit up the front steps of their house, enhancing the thick fog the evening brought with it. Of course, she knew he was home because his truck was parked to the side, but she didn't know how mad he was. *The nerve,* he thought to himself. *I came home early, and she wasn't even here to greet me.*

Footsteps were obvious on the wooden porch, and Geneva flung open the door, bright eyes and all smiles, there she stood with bags in hand, four or five at least, and her purse hung on her left shoulder. It was obvious she went on a shopping spree, something she loved to do. It was one of few things that gave her joy and it showed on her face. But Elijah was still mad.

Before he thought, "Where have you been? And why are you so late?" Elijah interrogated, being firm in his tone and his expression.

She dropped her bags on the floor and let her purse fall with them, and those fists of hers were like iron plopping down on her hips like they always did when she got mad. Elijah could hear her breathing, which wasn't a good thing. Her contented demeanor turned quickly. Step by step toward him, she finally stopped.

"Elijah James," swinging her finger in his face. "What are you doin' comin' in here and askin' me such a thing? I'm here by myself all day every day and I wanted to get out and do somethin'. I like to shop and so I did. I have some friends who like to shop, so they went with me. I spent a bunch a money and will do it again tomorrow if I want to. Do you have anything else to say?"

Losing the irritated look, he had when she first stepped in, replacing it with a small chuckle, then a belting laugh, he picked her up and whirled her around and around in front of the doorway.

"Elijah," she hollered out. "What in tarnation has gotten into you? You on drugs or somethin'? My lands, what in the world."

Elijah, still laughing, it carried over to her and she joined in, both seeing how silly they had been acting. Still holding her in his arms, he took advantage of the moment and gave one long, lingering kiss, making up for the time he was gone. They were joined as one person, embracing one another, making the best of a moment that could've gone the other way. Then he put her down.

"Where's Ella?" he asked, looking around.

"She stayed with a friend last night. You know she's fifteen now and wants to feel like she's grown," she said, "Now, let me show you what I bought," excitement oozing out of her." Oh, my goodness honey, the deals I got. I got a new bible case. You know my bible is gettin' worn. It was my mama's you know. I bought a few new clothes. A girl's always gotta have new clothes…"

Elijah followed her upstairs to their room, listening while she went on and on about her day's shopping adventure, and watched her pull one thing after another out of the sacks she totted in. From clothes to jewelry and a few nick knacks to boot. Normally he would interrupt, not interested, but he knew her angry side and he sure didn't want to rile it up.

Basking in the moment, a good moment at that, he woke up to the smell of Sunday breakfast, that scent floating all around him. His visions kept a smile on his face, leading him into the day at hand. Ella had sure gotten him spoiled, cooking the meals, and serving him like he was royalty or something, but he knew it wouldn't last forever. He also knew he would enjoy it for as long as it lasted. If he learned anything the night before, he learned to treasure every moment. He thought about how much he dwelled on negative things instead of things he should be thankful for. Although a few unwanted things still lingered in his mind, he wanted to get rid of, he figured it would take time.

"Dad," Ella yelled from the bottom of the stairs. "Breakfast is just about ready."

"Okay," Elijah answered loudly, getting up and putting on some warm flannel pants. "I'll be right down."

Elijah could hear the train in the distance but sounded like it ran right close to the house instead. That sound rang familiar to him, always living close enough to a track to hear that loud whistle blow since he was just a little boy. Each of those places held memories he knew his aging mind would never forget. Sitting there, letting his thoughts run away with him once more…he heard another voice hollering out.

"Pop," Caleb said, hearing his steps coming closer. "You better get down here before I eat up all of the hash browns. You know how I love homemade hash browns."

"Not as much as I do," Elijah replied, feeling spry, he jetted for the stairs fast as he could go, but not too fast, aggravating Caleb. It's like he lost twenty years, somehow the feeling of being down was gone and was replaced with something more…positive.

"Pop's got energy today, Ella," Caleb said, huffing a little as he entered the kitchen.

"I beat you," Elijah laughed. "Well maybe not, but I tried."

Jimmy, sitting at the table, already started on his plate of Scrambled eggs, bacon, sausage, homemade biscuits, gravy, and hash browns. Ella served him first and was fixing everyone else's plates. Jimmy said something, but no one could understand him because his mouth was full to the brim.

"Jimmy," Brenda said. "Didn't your mama teach you it's rude to talk with your mouth full?"

"Yep," he answered, biscuits and gravy oozing from the corners of his mouth.

No one could help but laugh at his crazy antics. There was one thing about Jimmy everyone knew. If laughter was needed, he did the trick. Some folks saw it as annoying, but most knew his ways, always trying to find a light in any darkness. It was true he wasn't the best person at one time, but he changed in a way no one could believe. Suddenly, he started making a difference in people in a positive way, kind of like Geneva did.

"Mmmmmm," Caleb muttered, sopping his biscuits in gravy. "You outdid yourself Ella. You sure did."

"I'm glad you like it, but we all need to start getting ready for church. It doesn't start until ten-thirty, but we have a crew to share two bathrooms. And you know us girls get them first," Ella said smiling.

"You best get to getting ready then, "Elijah said. "Me and the boys will just sit down here and talk about you and make bets on how long it'll take you three to get dressed."

"Brenda takes the longest," Jimmy chuckled. "I promise you that."

Tom, with his very quiet demeanor, chimed in, "Bridget will probably give her a run for her money."

The guys were having a good time making useless small talk, the girls went to get ready and escape such foolish conversation. None of them really looked forward to leaving, but they couldn't stay forever. So, the thoughts of going back home got pushed aside, choosing to enjoy the now. Ella held onto the time spent with her aunt Brenda and Bridget. Bridget always had such strength in dealing with any situation. Battling a sickness, she wouldn't let win but had the faith to believe in God's plan. And Brenda always stood by her sister's side.

There's something about being a twin, Brenda would always say. *It's a closeness no one can explain. It's a blessing from God!*

Regardless, Ella was so happy to have them there, especially with everything happening and what may happen. The unknown was the hardest pill to swallow and at the moment, lots of unknowns were surrounding them all.

The girls, trying to finish getting ready, went to Ella's room, giving the guys their turn. They were doing their hair and makeup all perfectly, and the conversation started.

"How's brother really doing?" Brenda asked, curling her blonde hair.

"I guess he's okay," Ella answered in a bit of an unsure tone. "He misses her so much and so do I."

"Something tells me she's doing just fine," Bridget added. "Besides, as she would say, she is too dad blame ornery for someone to hurt."

Ella grinned slightly, "I'd like to think so," she replied, finishing dressing. "But I do have to prepare myself for the worst as bad as I hate to say it. I know she wouldn't be so pessimistic, but…"

"She sure wouldn't," Brenda said with energy. "Now Ella, I want you to say out loud…mama is okay."

"I can't," Ella said, shaking her head.

"Say it," Bridget continued. "Geneva is okay. We'll say it together."

All as one, they said it together and ended with a group hug, leaning on each other for the strength they needed and treasuring that very moment. It had been some time since they saw one other, and time would come when they would be apart again. But, as so many say, *everything happens for a reason.* Ella wasn't sure what God's plan was by taking her away from everyone who loved her, but with faith, she had to believe.

Of course, it didn't take long for the guys to get ready since they didn't have to go through the trouble of makeup and trying to look pretty like the girls, and right before ten o'clock, they were on their way.

"You ever been with mama to church?" Ella asked Elijah.

"I hate to say it, but no," he answered. "Not for her lack of trying though. She told me every Sunday, I needed to get up, but every Sunday, I slept in and would hear her driving away. After a while, she quit asking."

"That doesn't sound like mama," Ella remarked surprised. "That doesn't sound like her at all."

"Well," Elijah added. "She said she was praying for me and that the good Lord would get me up outa of that bed one day."

"Now that sounds like her," she smiled. "You sounded just like her."

"Now that's a compliment," Elijah said, looking up to see they were approaching the church Geneva talked so much about for so long...the cowboy church.

At the entrance stood an iron gate and some plants on either side of the drive directly off the road. To the left, was a large arena and a dirt driveway going to it and the church straight ahead. Signs lined the right side of the drive with messages on each of them and Elijah paid close attention to every detail, something he would've never done before.

The rain the night before showed in the parking area of the church with patches of mud. Everyone was careful where they parked, Ella found a spot to the left of the front door away on a patch of grass. Suddenly, Elijah started getting nervous.

"What if lightning strikes when I walk in there," he asked Ella in a comical way.

"Oh, dad," she said, brushing off such a crazy comment.

"I guess we'll just have to see," he said with a wink, getting out and slowly walking toward the church. "Let's go."

CHAPTER THIRTEEN

An eighteen-wheeler sat in the far corner of the lot right next to the fence around the back of the place, and three rows of vehicles on that side filled the space. Many of the guys were sporting their cowboy hats, jeans and boots as did some of the ladies as well and Elijah smiled and nodded at everyone when they spoke. So many friendly people in one place and when he reached the door, greeters were there to welcome him and the rest of his crew.

"Glad you could make it today," one man said, tipping his hat and giving them a sheet with church information, then looking at Elijah. "I don't believe I've seen you here before."

"I'm...I'm..." Elijah tried to speak, but Ella took over.

"Geneva's my mama and this is my dad Elijah," Ella spoke out. "Of course, you know Jimmy and Brenda," she said, motioning toward her aunt and uncle.

"How could I forget Jimmy?" he said, then looking back at Ella and her dad. "And no one could ever forget Miss Geneva. I know it's only been a month or two, but this place isn't the same without her. I swear, that energy she brought was unmistakable. We are thankful for her."

"What did she do here?" Elijah asked, wanting to know everything he could about the part of her life he chose not to be a part of for so long.

"Oh man, what didn't she do," he said, trying his best to describe her value to the church and everyone in it. "Anytime we needed food for a wedding, funeral, anything, she jumped right in to help. She greeted old and new people to the church with open arms, a smile, and that unique laugh of hers. It echoed clean through this place. Too much to mention, but there is surely a void here without a doubt. I'll be praying for you folks."

Then a lady hearing their conversation added, "And what I wouldn't give to hear her say, *well how are you a doin' Miss Judy. I got some of that there homemade soup and cracklin' corn-bread to go along with it for saddle up...*and her wonderful bear hug that always followed. Goes to show, you don't re-alize how much you'll miss someone until they're not here anymore. Well, anyway, I sure miss my Geneva."

"Wow," Elijah said, surprised at how many lives Geneva had truly touched. "I had no idea."

"She told us she was going to bring you some Sunday, and I guess in a way, she got you here. The Lord works in mysterious ways brother." the man said, shaking his hand firmly, smiling. "Enjoy the service."

"I guess she did," Elijah smiled, thinking this might've been her plan the entire time. He got to thinking she was in the back hiding and would jump out and surprise him when he least expected, but it was all a foolish thought. It did sound good though. He wanted nothing more than for her to show up and do everything they said she did around there, lighting up the place once again.

They all went inside and were greeted with smiles, hand-shakes, and some, with a hug whether they knew them or not. Elijah went along with it, and he could tell Ella was happy being where her mama always was on Sunday morn-ings and any other time she was needed.

The place was put together, mainly with wood and tin. Everywhere you looked it was either wood or tin, a country kind of place to say the very least. The character it reflected seemed full of acceptance for anyone who graced their door. Elijah, noticing each detail, looked back. Caleb followed behind until he saw a couple of ladies to the left giving out donuts, milk, juices, biscuits, and gravy. Ella could see it in his eyes even before he hustled over to that lady and kindly thanked her after getting his pick of what he wanted.

"You can't still be hungry," Elijah commented, only to see Jimmy over at the table doing the exact same thing, loading up. "Where do y'all put it?"

Tom, unable to stop smiling, laughed at Elijah's commentary, took Bridget's hand, and went to find a place for them to sit.

Elijah followed Tom, and the rest trailed behind, finding an empty row close to the front. Elijah wasn't sure about sitting that far up, but he wasn't in an arguing mood, so he complied with no dispute.

"How's this?" Tom asked, "We won't miss anything from here."

"Folks sure are friendly," Bridget added. "I haven't been here since Jimmy got baptized."

"When was that?" Elijah asked, surprised he missed so much. "How did I not know."

"Geneva was here?" Jimmy said. "She said she asked you and you didn't answer. Anyway, brother Todd got to me, and my old ways were gone. I found Jesus, finally. Kind of like that song *The Old Man is Dead*. That was me. And I appreciate him showing me the way. I don't attend here any longer and I'm happy where we're at, but this is where it all started for me. This is where my life really started."

Elijah sat there and thought how he could have missed so many important things by his selfish thinking and insolent disposition and he looked up. The big stage before him was beautiful. There were stairs going up on each side and places for all the band's instruments around it. To the left and right of the stage were two large projector screens, but most importantly, in the center of the wall sat something magnificent. It was a huge cross made from wood. Behind it, the lights highlighted the entirety of such an incredible sight. For some reason, it kept his attention, his eyes could barely look away like something was drawing him closer and closer.

About then, a fellow with jeans, a starched green and white shirt, and a cowboy hat, pulled his attention. He had a goatee and smiled like he was happy to see them.

"Hey Jim," he waved, then. "I don't think I know you. I'm brother Todd. Glad you could be with us today."

Ella stood up, "Brother Todd, I'm Ella, Geneva's daughter and this is my dad, Elijah."

"Well, what a pleasure you guys came today. We sure miss Mama G," he said, his smile getting brighter as he spoke.

"Mama G?" Elijah asked.

"Oh yeah," brother Todd answered. "Lots of folks here call her that. She's like the grandma to the little ones, mama to those who need one, and just plain ole' Geneva to the rest of us. There was always something about her that drew everyone close."

"I know what you mean," Elijah said, smiling, understanding exactly what he was talking about.

"I'll keep you guys in my prayers and thank you for coming today," he said, patting Elijah on the back and going to the next row, greeting everyone he could.

Once more, Elijah looked back at the cross directly in front of him, but where he had to look up. People were talking and visiting all around, but for some reason, he could hear a voice trying to tell him something. The glowing cross before him stood for more than just wood and lights. It was saying something else, but nothing seemed clear. He couldn't pinpoint the message.

"What do you think dad?" Ella slightly nudged him, still glancing around the room.

"Different."

"That's all you can say is different?" she continued.

"Well Ella," Elijah said. "It's not your usual, run-of-the-mill, traditional kind of church. I know that much."

"Exactly," Ella smiled. "That's why mama loved it so much. She wasn't your usual, run of the mill, traditional kind of gal either. Wouldn't you agree?"

"Point taken," he smiled, then noticed the band going onto the stage and getting in a circle to pray. Those who were still wandering around found their seats and got ready for the service.

Moments later, from the guitar to the harmonica, they began to play some traditional old hymns with a country gospel twist, giving it a different feel. Elijah remembered his grandmother listening to those same old songs, but somewhat different. The beat and instruments blended to where there were feet tapping and hand clapping to go along with the melody.

"Come on everybody, stand and let's worship the Lord together today. Ain't it good to be in the house of the Lord this mornin'," the singer announced with a country twang, motioning and everyone standing.

Jimmy, Brenda, Bridget, Tom, Ella, and Caleb, all looked like they were at a revival, their spirits being lifted by the music floating all around. And the feeling in the place was something Elijah had never experienced before. Never being a churchgoer, his expectations, as opposed to the reality of that day, were so completely different. He expected suits and ties, dresses, and straight-talking people, not the country way of life he always knew. The atmosphere put off a welcoming vibe that somehow, he thought, he might belong there.

"I love this," Ella told Elijah, getting right up in his ear so he could hear her.

Elijah gave an agreeing nod and sat down when the next song started. He could never picture himself enjoying such a thing as church or gospel music, but it touched him in ways he couldn't explain. After four or five worship songs, some old and some new country style with a Christian message, the words, and message in each song, hit a different part of everyone. That's when only the keyboard player was left, giving a slow melody for the preacher as he made his way to the pulpit.

For whatever reason, a part of him wanted to hear what that preacher had to say. Strange as it was, he sat there waiting for what knowledge that man would lay on him, knowing he needed every ounce of goodness he could grab a hold of.

"Take your bibles and turn to John chapter fifteen, starting in verse twelve, and please stand for the reading of God's word, in honor of him," he said. "It says *This is my commandment, that you love one another as I have loved you.* Kind of a rare thing in America, these days, it seems like."

Elijah listened closely to what brother Todd said next and it really caught his attention. They weren't only words, but the truth Geneva always spoke of.

Brother Todd said, "What he's sayin' here is to act like God does, not like the world. Don't stoop down to their level. *And the next verse says Greater love has no one than this, that someone lay down his life for his friends.*"

After the reading of such a scripture, the preacher began to pray *"Father, I ask you in the name of Jesus to bless the reading of your word. Let this not be a message that I speak. I pray in the name of Jesus that it be a message that you speak directly into our hearts. I pray you give us strength to follow you, to not be a coward. To stand up for you, in a world that is backing up from*

*you, doing a disgrace to you. Start with us here today...in Jesus'
name...AMEN."*

After bowing his head to pray as brother Todd asked,
Elijah sat in the moment, not in the past or the days to
come, but that very moment. The words he spoke, to not
be a coward, stuck out in his head, thinking that's what he
had been far too long. And the short prayer was powerful in
many ways.

Elijah looked over, and the three couples with him were
all leaning into one another, listening intensely to the message, and gave Elijah a lonely feeling inside. *I could've shared
this with Geneva,* he thought to himself.

"This series is called *A Better Way,"* brother Todd said.
*"There is hope...there is a better way. Jesus said in this scripture
that you need to live his way...you see he gave his life for you,
and we all need to give our life to him. He says love others like I
love you."*

Elijah listened to the preacher's talk about love, and
he thought and thought about the many times he had the
chance to show love when all he gave was bitterness and
anger. So many times, choosing love would've been so much
easier and more accepted, but something inside of him, kept
up a wall of resentment, keeping him from doing the right
thing.

Brother Todd continued and had Elijah's complete attention, hanging on every word.

"War scars a man," brother Todd continued. "America
is at war. There is a war going on for the souls of mankind
and hanging in the balance between imprisonment and hell
with Satan and his warriors, and a glorious inheritance in
Heaven. Hanging in the balance between that is you and
me. Our commander in chief, left us with a job to do, that
many of us have gotten so busy, we have abandoned our post.

The enemy is using things to distract us and keep us busy and pushed away from God."

Everything he said, hit the nail on the head for Elijah. With all his talk about being too busy all the time, never taking time for what matters in life, hit Elijah in the center of his heart. Knowing he always put unimportant things before the things that mattered, began to convict him like never before.

Looking around, seeing everyone, their focus straight ahead, feeling a power that was indescribable. Something inside of him, a welling up of peace and love, started to fill the emptiness and void.

The preacher turned to another scripture, "In Ephesians chapter six verse twelve…God Begins to explain this war in America. *For we do not wrestle against flesh and blood, but against the rulers, against the authorities, against cosmic powers over his present darkness, against the spiritual forces of evil in the Heavenly places.* What he's saying here is that Satan has these rulers that are in command that are here to disrupt everything we are doing to keep us from being on the right side."

I was supposed to be here Geneva, Elijah thought to himself. *I have been the devil. I've been living the way of the world.*

Elijah, hanging on every word this powerful preacher threw at him, and it was like everything he talked about applied to him. It's like he was talking directly to Elijah James, a devilish man who lived his whole life with no thoughts of God and a higher power. Every analogy fit perfectly and every bit of anger he always held in, begin to float out of his body, being replaced with something sacred.

Then, at the end of the service, brother Todd read one final scripture, "In John chapter fourteen verse six, it says *Jesus said to him, I am the way, the truth, and the life. No one comes to the Father except through me.* You see, you have to choose which side you're going to be on today. Choose which commander in chief you're going to follow. Choose…"

Then the final prayer came…everyone's head bowed, "*Father give us the strength where we have chosen the ways of the world. We've been so busy. We're complaining about what's going on, but we're not in the fight. We're too busy. We're the ones that need to be rescued. We are busy following the things of the world and not a soldier for Jesus. Lord forgive us. Lord because we're so busy, we'll die and wake up in Hell with general Satan and his troops in a lake of fire. If that's you today, I'm not talking about what somebody thinks about you or what your spouse thinks about you…or what I think about you. When God looks at you, have you deserted his purpose and his calling in your life? Maybe you need to repent and turn around. There's gotta be some changes. Under your commander Jesus Christ. Somehow you slipped to the wrong side, and you didn't even know it. Ask God, please forgive me. I have deserted you. Can I humbly come back to you and ask in the name of Jesus to be one of your soldiers? Maybe today you need to accept Jesus. Just ask him, please God forgive me. You gave your life for me, and I want to give my life to you. Fill me with your presents with the holy spirit. Use me in the fight. I now commit to follow you Jesus…Amen*

Elijah, leaned forward, resting his elbows on his knees, his hands covering his face, staying like that even after the prayer was over.

"Dad," Ella said, putting her arm around him, but the look on his face when he sat up and turned to her was unmistakable. It was a moment she had prayed for.

CHAPTER FOURTEEN

Tears were streaming down Elijah's face as Ella had never seen before, but sadness isn't what showed amid such tears. Unhappiness was nowhere in sight. Instead, she saw a glow about him. His eyes were brighter than ever and the smile within his tears highlighted only one thing. The more he wiped away, it seemed a hundred more rolled down. It was like all the things he had done in the past were being cried out and wiped away before her eyes. The feeling around them was nothing short of spiritual and all she could do was give him a sincere embrace, sharing a moment she would never forget.

"Pop," Caleb muttered softly, leaning over, and joining in on such an embrace, while the others looked on.

"I said the prayer with brother Todd," Elijah said, his words somewhat broken up with the emotion flowing out of him. "I talked to God."

A feeling of thankfulness and blessing, came over Ella, hearing such words from her dad's lips. And for a moment, she didn't know what to say, almost sure what he was trying to tell her.

"You always said God didn't know who you were dad," Ella smiled, wiping tears.

"That wasn't true Ella," Elijah answered, smiling. "I didn't know him, but I do now."

Jimmy, overhearing what was being said, stood there full of emotion. Years before, no one would've ever caught him showing anything like that, but the spirit surrounding them, took over. It filled every nook and cranny where any negative thoughts or past sins dwelled and changed them into hope for a future God meant for them.

Brother Todd had just finished praying with a young couple and, without another word, Elijah stood up and went in his direction. Everyone else stayed where they were, knowing it was something he had to do, but they watched, taking in such a miracle before their eyes. They watched them join hands and pray together, what felt like five minutes long, but considering everything, it made sense. And when he was done, they both walked over.

"Looks like we got a new brother in Christ y'all," brother Todd said, grinning ear to ear, then turning to Elijah. "I'm proud of you brother. Geneva would be proud too. I can promise you that."

"Thank you, sir," Elijah nodded. "I hope you're right. I've always wanted to make her proud, but…"

"Now, you've made us all proud," Ella broke in. "We all love you so much."

"See you next Sunday," brother Todd asked, a question mark at the end of the sentence, hoping the answer was *yes*.

Reaching out and shaking his hand, Elijah gave a big smile, "See you next Sunday pastor."

Elijah and the rest made their way to their vehicles, speaking to everyone still hanging around and visiting, Ella held to her dad's hand tightly. The chill in the air encouraged them to hurry and get in their cars to get home.

"The first thing I'm going to do when we get home, is build a fire," Caleb said, rubbing his hands together like you would two sticks in the woods to make flames. "And cuddle with my honey."

"Caleb, stop it," Ella said, grinning like a young girl getting a compliment from a crush. "You're so sweet."

"I swear, you two are something else," Elijah said, resting his head back, trying his best to take in what just happened.

Elijah let the events of the day sink in, and it seemed impossible. He thought to himself, how can one sermon, one day in church, one country preacher, turn him around so easily. How could all the years he spent bitter and angry be wiped away with a simple prayer? His mind was going here and there, then he relaxed, listening to Ella and Caleb make small talk all the way home. Their customary banter got to be usual, but entertaining thing to listen to. Ella was easy to aggravate, and Caleb darn sure loved doing it. Regardless, if there ever was a perfect pair, it was those two. The love they shared could be seen a mile away. Although Ella was sometimes spirited and stubborn like her mother, she also had the same heart.

"We're about home," Caleb said, steadily teasing Ella the entire drive.

Jimmy said they were going to stop and pick up something up for lunch and bring it back to the house. Elijah knew they would be heading back to Dallas that evening and wanted to make sure he didn't take a minute for granted. He wanted to enjoy it while they were there. When he was younger, he hated to admit it, but he was like Caleb, picking and aggravating those twin sisters of his every chance he got. It was just the thing to do.

Finally making it back, Caleb jumped out and ran around to open Ella's door then dashed for the front door. "Come on Pop," he said. "It's cold out here."

Elijah laughed at him and took his own sweet time up the steps, "It's not that cold," he said, opening the door and watching Caleb head straight for the fireplace to get a flame going.

"I don't know what I'm gonna do with him," Ella said, following behind. "I swear sometimes he acts just like a kid, but then…"

"He's pretty great," Elijah finishing her sentence. "You're lucky Ella. I'm glad you have each other."

Ella agreed with a sincere gesture, and she went in to enjoy the warmth from the fire, sitting on the thick comfy rug and Caleb joining her once the fire was blazing. About then, the small flip phone Elijah always carried around, but seldom used, began to ring. He did his best to dig it out before it stopped, "Hello," he answered.

"Elijah, this is Sheriff Talley," she said. "Did I catch you at a bad time?"

"Just waiting on Jimmy to get back with lunch," Elijah said, a little nervous, afraid to even ask why she was calling in the first place, letting silence prevail.

"Can you come to the sheriff's office over on seventy-one highway, later this evening, maybe around 4. It should be here by then," she stated, business-like but with her normal, kind and caring way at the same time.

"What should be there?" Elijah asked, already knowing what she was talking about.

"Geneva's car," she answered. "They're a few hours out, but just whenever you want to come after three o'clock would be fine. We thought you might want to be here."

"I do," he said, trying not to let the sadness he was feeling, creep into the joy he just experienced. "Have you gotten any more information at all?"

"All we know is that some guy, described in his twenties, abandon it in Baton Rouge. A few people came forward, but none of the descriptions different people gave, were the same, so there's nothing concrete to go on."

"Nancy," he said as sincerely as he could, normally not calling her by her first name. "We have to find her. Whatever the outcome, I have to know what happened to her... please."

"You know I loved her too," Sheriff Talley replied, showing her heart in such kind words. "She was special to everybody. You couldn't help but love her, being so dad blame funny, crazy, and inspiring all wrapped up into one spitfire of an old lady. What can I say Elijah, if anyone could find a way to survive anything, I'd bet on Geneva any day of the week. Keep your head up and keep hope. I'll see you this afternoon."

Elijah hung up the phone, trying to keep the call to himself for the time being, and went to make a glass of tea, joining Ella and Caleb in the living room. They were huddle together, both looking toward the fire. The heat from it, floated all around the room, taking any chill lingering before. He sat down to enjoy the peacefulness of the moment and couldn't help but smile from the inside out. He knew where he had to go later that evening, but it didn't change the miracle he experienced in the middle of that country church at the edge of town. He knew, no matter the outcome of what he finds out, the woman he was led to marry, helped him find the right path even if she wasn't there any longer. Something about it was a miracle, but the memories etched in the depths of his mind would live on forever.

"I'm home," Jimmy's voice rang out as the front door flung open, his crew following behind.

"Brother, we got a good ole country dinner, fried chicken," Bridget said, helping to tote in the mess of food they brought.

"I call the legs," Caleb hollered out, jumping up and leaving Ella sitting on the rug by herself.

"Caleb," Ella said, pretending to be angry.

Caleb replied smiling back at her, "Sorry honey, you know how I love drumsticks."

Having that many people there, somehow gave Elijah a sense of peace even though there were many unknowns to come and watching them snatch and grab this and that in the kitchen brought back old times when they were younger.

Elijah joined them in the kitchen and saw a nice spread. There was chicken, baked beans, potatoes, rolls, and a couple of sweet potato pies to boot. Caleb tried, but Jimmy grabbed a few legs from the box. For a minute, they looked like they were going to fight over such an insignificant thing, but in the end, they were just picking at each other as always.

"Mmmm," Caleb said, taking a bite while caring his plate into the living room. "You better hurry Pop before it's all gone." Then turning to Ella, "Will you grab my tea please?"

Elijah waited until the wild animals cleared and went to see what remained. He fixed himself a small plate, knowing he wouldn't eat it if he piled it too high, and went to join the rest. Everyone found a spot in the living room since it was the warmest place, and Elijah did the same, setting his plate down.

For a few moments, there was no chatter because their mouths were full, but the minute, they could, words were flying around.

"I remember back in the day," Elijah thought back. "We were pretty poor, and we mostly ate beans and cornbread."

"That's right brother," Brenda added. "And sometimes mama would bring home one chicken, a small one at that. It sure was hard splitting a small chicken five ways since daddy usually got the most part of it."

"Wait a minute now," Elijah said. "If I remember correctly, you two were the babies and got anything you wanted. You would always flash your pretty blue eyes at mama and daddy and fling that blonde hair of yours and that's all she wrote."

Brenda and Bridget looked at one another and started to laugh, "We didn't get our way all the time," Brenda said. "Just most of it."

Jimmy couldn't stand it, he wanted his say even though it didn't have to do with their life, he had a story to tell. He was chomping at the bits to jump in.

"My little sister always got me in trouble for something I didn't do, so one day I got her back," Jimmy said, giving a tiny evil grin. "Me and my best friend Tony were going to do something, and she said she was going to tell daddy, so we took care of that."

"What did you do? Kill her," laughed Caleb.

"We had this tree in our back yard down the hill from the house," Jimmy continued. "We tied her upside down in that tree and put a barrel of water underneath her so if she fell, she'd get drenched."

"That was mean," Bridget said. "I bet you got in trouble anyway."

"I did. We left her there and went back to school for football practice and then the game," he replied, nodding his head. "And during the game, I looked up and my mama was pointing at me. I looked at Tony and said, *'man I think you're in trouble.'*"

"You could've killed her," Elijah said, his face showing shock from such a crazy story.

"We didn't think about that back then Eli," he said. "We didn't think about the blood going to her head or anything. I just got tired of her always trying to get me in trouble and for once they punished me for something I did do. Felt kind of good."

"Whatever happened to your best friend," Elijah asked. "Tony."

"He married my sister," Jimmy said. "Talk about a turn of events huh. I guess she figured if he tied her up in a tree, he liked her. Who knows?"

Jimmy never failed to give us the humor we needed to break up the tension of any kind. In fact, I always remember when Geneva would be a little down for whatever reason, and she would say, "Elijah, I need Jimmy and Brenda to come to visit. That Jimmy is downright crazy, but I love 'em. One thing's for sure…he makes me laugh. And laughter cures a lot these days."

"By the way," Ella asked. "Who called a bit ago? Your phone doesn't ring very much and by the way, you need to get an updated phone. That flip phone thing is outdated."

"Them blame new-fangled phones confuse me and I don't need to do anything but make and answer calls. I don't take pictures or get on those social sites like you youngsters do, so there," he remarked, trying to dodge the main question about who called.

"Alright then, but who was it?" she asked once more.

Elijah got up and walked to the kitchen, "It was Sheriff Tally."

By the time he got in the kitchen, like magic, they all appeared behind him, every eye staring at him, and listening for him to finish.

"Alright, alright," he said. "Geneva's car will be at the sheriff's office soon and the sheriff thought I might want to be there."

They all began to talk simultaneously where not a single word was understandable.

"Wait," Elijah said, raising his voice to get their attention. "I get it. We'll all go."

It was a little before two o'clock and they still had an hour or so before she said to come. Jimmy, Brenda, Tom, and Bridget went to gather their things and put them in their car, so they would be ready when they had to leave. In a way, Elijah wished they could stay that way, always having family around, but he knew it wasn't real. They all had lives to live, and he had to learn to live best he could.

When the time came to go to the sheriff's department, Elijah stood in front of the table in the entryway, staring at a few pictures. One, was of him and Geneva on their wedding day and the other was of him and Geneva sitting on the front porch, about six months earlier. Geneva's smile gleamed as always, but Elijah's smile, not so authentic.

"You ready dad?" Ella asked, looping her arm in his.

"You see this," he asked, pointing a the most recent photo.

"What about it?" she said. "It's a great picture. I took it. Remember dad?"

"I remember, but that's not what I'm talking about," he continued.

"Then what?"

"You see her smile? She always wore it even in the worst of times, even when we didn't have two nickels to rub together, it was always there. Then look at me," he said, shaking his head in regret.

"Dad," she said. "We need to go."

Elijah picked up the picture, "If I had her here now, I promise you, I would put on a real smile like I should have that day. I didn't know how lucky and how blessed I really was."

No longer rushing him, she turned him to her. "All we can do now is look ahead. I heard someone say once if you keep looking back, you can never move forward. We all need to move forward, and we don't know God's plan. We just have to have faith and believe everything will be as he wants it to be."

"You know what Ella," Elijah smiled. "A while back, I would've told you, that was a bunch of malarky, but I believe it now. Let's go."

They all got in two different cars as before and played follow the leader to the sheriff's office. Every minute, the closer they got, Elijah's heart pounded harder and faster, petrified of what news he would get when they arrived. So many thoughts were running rampant through his mind, it was hard for him to organize them in any fashion. All he knew is, he wanted to find Geneva. Memories of her stayed constant in his head, trying all he could not forget a single time they spent together, even the bad times. Then Caleb took the last turn, then into the driveway of their destination. Elijah took in a long breath and let it out slowly, he did all he could to slow his heartbeats, so he didn't feel like he was having a heart attack.

"We're here Pop," Caleb said, turning around to him. "Are you okay?"

"I suppose," Elijah said, fighting the anxiety attacking him.

"Are you sure you want to do this?" Ella added, reaching back and grasping his hand.

"I have to," Elijah Answered, squeezing her hand. "We have to."

Jimmy and the rest pulled up soon after, got out and they all started toward the front door of the sheriff's office.

CHAPTER FIFTEEN

They walked into the building, and Elijah remembered how the front room always looked, bland to say the very least, but then again, people were brought there to be locked up, so it was to be expected. There were only a few people sitting in the chairs lined up in front of one of the windows where tickets were paid. Other than that, there wasn't much going on.

Elijah started toward the lady behind the glass where the sheriff was, and he felt a tap on the shoulder. At first, he thought it was Caleb, aggravating once more, then turned around starting to say something.

"What in the world are you doing here Eli," an old friend said, Terry Larey, a local bail bondsman, Elijah had known since he was a kid. "You're not in trouble are ya," he asked, laughing. "If you are, I'll get you out."

Terry was one of the few people who ever called him Eli, but it was okay. Since they were kids, Terry always had his back. After a while, Terry didn't hang out with Elijah much because of his troublemaking ways back then. Terry was always one of those Christian boys, but to Elijah, he was always a friend no matter what. In those days, everyone knew Elijah wasn't much of a God person, but Terry always tried to be a good influence on him regardless. It's something he always remembered about Terry.

"I'm a...well, I'm meeting sheriff Talley here," Elijah said, stuttering a bit. "She..."

Terry put his hand on Elijah's shoulder, "I know all about it, Eli," he said. "I talk to Nancy quite often and she knows what a history you and I have and thought I might need to be here for support. I hope you don't mind her telling me. Besides, anything I can do to help, I will. You know that."

"That's how you've always been," Elijah smiled. "Even when I was at my worst, you were there."

"I'm still here," he said, then looking toward Brenda and Bridget. "I haven't seen you two since God knows when. And I'm guessing these two are the ones who put up with you now."

"Don't start Terry," Brenda laughed. "The truth is, we put up with them."

They made small talk for a minute and could see the sheriff through the window.

Terry motioned to everyone, "Now let's go and see if we can piece together this Geneva puzzle and find that woman. How does that sound Eli?"

"Sounds great to me," Elijah replied, following behind him to the doors heading into the main office. "She's not getting away with leaving me."

"You mean ole goat, I'm surprised she didn't leave you years ago, but she loved you so blame much," Terry said, steadily walking toward Nancy standing by her office door.

"They dropped it off a bit ago and we've gone through it already, but I figured you would want to do the same," sheriff Talley said, leading in the direction of where they needed to go, making a few turns down the hallway, then outside.

In the corner of the lot, there it sat, Geneva's red dodge caravan. Other than being a bit dirty, which is not how she took care of it, nothing looked out of sorts.

"You all look through it to see if you find something we might've missed, " the sheriff said, her blue eyes motioning everyone to follow. She gave everyone a pair of clear gloves, like a doctor would wear. "Put these on. We wouldn't want to mess up any evidence if there's any left, now, would we?"

Everyone did as she asked and took a section to search, hoping to find something, anything to lead them to where she was when it happened. Ella and Caleb took the back, although there wasn't much of anything there. Terry started on the left side of the back seat, while the sheriff was on the right side. Elijah opened the front car door and sat down in the seat, looking left, right, up, and down, for any indication of where they could go to look for her. When Terry got in on the rider's side, he looked in the floorboard first.

"Look," Terry said, holding up a bag. "Is this her purse?"

"Looks like it," Elijah said, staring carefully at it, considering he never paid much attention to details like that.

"There's not much in it," he said. "Wallet's been cleaned out like it's never been used. Whoever did this probably emptied it out and just took whatever cash she had."

Elijah started feeling very overwhelmed, letting many different scenarios race in and out of his mind, thinking the worst, and starting to hyperventilate. He started feeling like he couldn't breathe and grabbed his chest, praying God would help him calm down.

"Call 911," Terry yelled out, not knowing if Elijah was having a heart attack, and ran to his side, doing all he could to calm him down. "Eli, just breathe slowly. In through your nose, out through your mouth, very slow. Come on now my friend. You're gonna be just fine," Terry said.

"Geneva," he said, then losing consciousness.

"Dad," Ella screamed, rushing over by his side as Terry found a spot on the ground to lay him, waiting on the EMTs. "Wake up dad."

Everyone encircling him, everyone made way for the paramedics when they arrived only a few short moments later. It didn't take them long to get him conscious once more and gave him something to calm him down.

"You had a severe anxiety attack, sir," the paramedic said, steadily checking him.

In a weak tone, Elijah asked, "What's your name?"

"Monty sir and I'm going to take good care of you," he said. "Just take slow breathes…what's your name?"

"Elijah," he said, breathing slow like he asked.

"Nice to meet you Elijah," Monty said, not ceasing his treatment, checking his blood pressure and whatever else he needed to do. "You have lots of people who care."

"God cares too," Elijah said, not expecting that to come out of his mouth.

Monty stopped for a moment and took Elijah's hand, "Yes he does sir. He cares about us all."

"You married son?" Elijah asked, calming down more and more by the minute, the medication finally taking effect.

"Yes, sir I am. Her name is Christi," Monty answered with a big smile on his face.

"Treasure her. Love her," Elijah continued. "You never know when your time is up."

"I do sir and I love her very much and my girls," he replied, checking his vitals once more.

"I have a girl," Elijah said, pointing to Ella. "She's beautiful, isn't she?"

"Yes sir, she is," Monty said, glancing at Ella and back at him. "You're a lucky man."

Without a word, he gave an agreeing nod and smile. Then he realized they were putting him on a stretcher. One thing he didn't want to do, was leave that place. He needed to find out where Geneva was, and that car was their only clue.

"No, I have to stay here," Elijah said, steadily trying to get up. "Nancy, Terry, tell them, I have to stay."

Terry went to Elijah before they put him in the ambulance, and said, "What you have to do, is get checked out Eli.

Now, Nancy and I will go through every inch of this here car, while you get a once over at the hospital. You hear me?"

"That's right dad," Ella said, coming to his other side. "We'll follow and meet you there."

"It's just precautionary," Monty said. "Just making sure there aren't any heart issues. If not, you'll be out in a jiffy Elijah. I promise."

"I'm going to hold you to that," Elijah replied, looking him directly in the eyes.

They loaded him into the ambulance and the others followed while Terry and the sheriff continued to search for anything to guide them. On the way, they gave him one more injection, one to make him rest, and it did. Before he knew it, his eyes were closed, and his thoughts landed far from there, bringing back a memory he thought he'd forgotten.

"Elijah honey, ain't you ready yet," Geneva grumbled. "I'm ready to dance and that there band is about the best around, country band anyway. And you know that's all I like. I love me some country. Hurry up now."

"I'm trying Geneva," Elijah answered. "I'm trying to get these blame jeans buttoned you told me to wear. I swear I feel like I've been poured in them."

"Gotta wear pants like that when we go boot-scootin' honey. Everybody knows that" Geneva laughed. "Besides, you look good in them there things."

"If I could breathe, I'd be alright," Elijah said, finally getting them buttoned and putting his belt on. "I don't understand Geneva. You don't drink and they drink there."

"You ain't gotta drink to dance honey. How many times do I gotta tell you that? I know you done figured out it don't do no good to argue with me," she said, grabbing up her coat and purse and jetting out the door.

Elijah did his best to keep up with her, shutting and locking the door. Since Ella was finally grown and in college, their schedule seemed busier than before she left. It was like Geneva wanted to go all the time. Elijah's attitude wasn't always the best, but he went along with her most of the time.

When they arrived at the dance hall, that's what Geneva called it, they got out. The music was on the inside, but it rang clear to the parking lot, so much to where you could dance out there. Still trying to keep up with her, he took double steps to do so.

"You're slower than a Sunday afternoon honey, come on," she said, reaching the door.

It swung open, almost hitting her. The guy going out was a big burly type. He had a long thick beard and wore a leather vest. He was tall as a mountain, but when he greeted Geneva, he was different.

"I'm so sorry Geneva, I hope I didn't hit you," he said.

"You didn't Dude," Geneva smiled. "You leavin' already?"

"Yes ma'am," he said. "We have a fundraiser to do tomorrow with the Bearded Sinners and I can't be late."

"Good luck," she said, making her way inside.

"Dude," he asked Geneva.

"It's his name silly," she said. "He's a good guy. They do a lot for people. We need more people like him."

Geneva changed gears and slapped a few bucks on the counter to pay our way in and went through the swinging door to the other side. That place was full of people, some drinking, some not, but they all seemed to be having one heck of a time. The old country-style music blared throughout the place as folks danced the two-step and the waltz. They found a table closest to the dancefloor, but there was a couple already there. About the only two seats left open in the place were with them.

"You mind if we join you," Geneva asked, energy exuding from her.

The couple looked at each other then, "Not at all. Have a seat. I'm Charlie, and this is my husband, Jerry."

"Nice to meet you, folks," Geneva answered. "And this Elijah."

"Her husband," Elijah added.

"Yeah, yeah, my husband," Geneva said, giving her little hehe laugh she always did when she was doing her best to aggravate.

They made small talk the best they could, considering the music was so loud, they could barely hear themselves think, but it seemed Geneva and Charlie became fast friends. From whispering in each other's ear to laughing out loud, neither Jerry nor Elijah had a clue what they were talking about, but then again, they figured it didn't matter.

"Come on honey," Geneva said, grabbing Elijah's hand. "Let's cut a rug."

"But..." Elijah started to say, although she had already drug him out on the dance floor juking and a jiving to one of those Hank Williams Jr tunes.

It wasn't long, Jerry and Charlie joined them. With the dance floor packed, it was hard to move around, but they made their way around it, no problem. Geneva's enthusiasm poured out with every step, twisting, and turning, she had perfect rhythm to the music the band was playing.

"I have to sit down Geneva," Elijah said. "You're about to tire me out."

After hours of dancing and visiting with their newfound friends, they left heading home. On the drive, Geneva admitted something she hadn't before.

"Elijah, remember when I told you I tried to poison my grandpa," she asked as he would ever forget such a thing.

"Well, I got to thinkin' 'bout that one day, knowin' I would stand before God and give account for what I tried to do, so I wrote grandpa a letter and told him what I'd done," she said, not sure why she was telling it right then and there. "Anyway, he wrote me back and said sometimes in life we all do somethin' we're a sorry for, and he even sent me a New Testament bible,"

"The one in the dresser drawer," he asked, surprised at such a story.

"You betcha," she said. "Just thought I'd tell ya that so you wouldn't think I was gonna try to kill ya sometime."

"Why would I think that?" he asked, a little afraid to ask such a question. And she just laughed. About then they hit a huge pothole jarring them for a moment, the very moment reality kicked in and pulled him from that place in time.

"Sorry about that Elijah," Monty said, the ambulance bouncing around after hitting a bad spot in the road just before pulling into the hospital emergency drive.

The meds he'd been given, were still working and his heart was no longer pulsating a hundred miles an hour like it was. Instead, it had a slow and steady pace as his breathing had normalized.

"He we go," Monty said, rolling him into the emergency room entrance. "They're going to look you over and make sure nothing alarming is going on and I'm sure they'll let you go home. It's been a pleasure taking care of you sir."

"Thank you," Elijah said, then surprising himself, ask the kind paramedic, "Will you pray for me and my wife, Geneva, that we find her. I can tell you talk to God a lot.

"I'd be honored," he said, placing his hand on Elijah's. *"Dear Heavenly Father, we ask for your help today. Please wrap your arms around Elijah, aid in his healing Lord, and give him peace. Lord, I don't know Geneva or where she is, or what's going on, but you do. Please give guidance in this situation, always*

*letting them feel your love through it all. Be with this family. I
ask this is Jesus' name...AMEN."*

When he was finished, it left Elijah with a smile across
his face as Monty walked away, turning back once with a big
grin. Then someone else took over and wheeled him into a
room. Elijah hated the feel and the smell of hospitals. It's
something he hated from when he was younger and had to
visit a relative. He always stayed as far from hospitals as he
could, but suddenly, he had no choice.

It was only a few minutes before his entire crew was
there to join him. He could hear Jimmy and Caleb from
down the hallway, doctors and nurses turning to see what
the clamor was. The girls automatically did their job, toning
them down and they came in the room. There were only
three chairs, so the girls took them, leaving the guys leaning
against the wall.

"They're gonna run us out," Jimmy said, his funny grin
showing.

"As loud as you are, I don't blame them, Uncle Jimmy,"
Ella said, shaking her head, looking over at Brenda as to say
how do you put up with him.

Elijah kept his eyes on the door, waiting for a nurse or
doctor to come in and make sure he was okay, so they could
take him home, but that's not who he saw walking in.

CHAPTER SIXTEEN

The sheriff and Terry walked in gingerly like they were trying to make sure they didn't wake me. Elijah had only been settled in no longer than thirty minutes or so, and his curiosity overwhelmed his thoughts, some of them, thinking the worst. Ella and Caleb, sitting on each side of him, got up to let them have a seat.

"How you feelin' Eli?" Terry asked, giving the friendly grin he always wore. "I knew you were too dang mean for anything to happen to you."

"I'll second that," the sheriff said.

"I'm feeling okay, and I appreciate the small talk and all," Elijah started. "But I can tell you two are dancing around something you want to tell me and I'm an impatient man. So go ahead and spill it. Whatever you have to say, you can say in front of my family. They all want to know just like me."

"Alright then Elijah, "Nancy said. "It didn't take long to go through Geneva's car. You know she's always been neat as a pin. There was nothing in the back or back seat, and, at first, we didn't think we'd find anything..."

"But..." Elijah said, coaxing her to finish, knowing there was more to tell. "What did you find? I can handle whatever it is."

Ella took a step toward them, "Do you know where my mama is? Please say you do," she spoke up, carrying her emotions on her sleeve for all to see.

"Not exactly," Terry replied, obviously holding something behind his back.

"What do you have?" Elijah sat up best he could, trying to see. "Come on Terry."

Bringing his hand forward, he was holding several bags. One was pink with three crosses on it and a name of a business no one heard of, and the other was cloth white with an outline of a bible on the front. Terry set one down and opened the other. He pulled out a cross much resembling the one she used to have when she was younger, except it was one you would hang on the wall. It was different but still had hints of turquoise stones in a cross pattern on a wooden background. That was always her favorite color. Next, he lifted out a devotional, with a calendar of daily things to read and a place for notes. One thing she always loved, was devotionals. She probably had dozens, but at one time or another, she read them all.

"What's in the other bag?" Elijah asked just as Terry reached for it.

"Eli," Terry said solemnly, "She loved you very much."

"I know that Terry, but what's in the bag?" Elijah demanded, but in a most respectful way.

Lifting out a box containing a bible, he handed it to Elijah, "Open it, Eli."

At first, Elijah just stared at it, not removing the top just yet. By holding it, something made him feel close to her.

"Open it, dad," Ella said, going to his side, rubbing his arm to show her support.

"I'm afraid to," Elijah muttered. "What if…"

"I'm here dad," Ella said. "I'll always be here. It's important to see what's inside."

"Okay honey," he said, looking Ella in the eyes then back to the bible case.

Terry lifted the lid off slowly, and inside, was a magnificent bible. It was a soft brown leather cover with unique etchings outlining it front and back. On the front, a cross with the same etchings surrounded it. Below the cross, it read "Family Bible." And below that engraved was *Elijah James, The James Family*. Elijah felt every inch of the bible, the softness of the leather massaging his fingertips and the smell of it reminded him of something familiar. Then he opened it. On the first page, it said, presented to Elijah James, my love, by Geneva James, your wife. But when he got to the next line, he looked up at the sheriff and Terry.

"She dated it," he said. "Sheriff, she dated it."

"We know," the sheriff said. "That gives us something to go on."

"But we don't know where to start," Elijah added, letting his joy from such a gift, turn grim instantly.

"Not exactly my friend," Terry replied, giving his, up to something kind of look, then pulling a receipt from out of both bags with a timestamp and store she bought both items. "She went to Shreveport, Eli. She bought these things in Shreveport."

"She said she wanted to go shopping, but she didn't say in Shreveport," Elijah muttered."

"Did you ask where she wanted to go?" Terry replied. "That day she left, did you ask her where she wanted to go?"

Without answering, Elijah only shook his head, tightly holding the incredible gift in his lap. Everyone let silence have its way for a few moments, letting him come to grips with the reality of the situation.

"Now we know where to start and we have a date, we can get to searching. How does that sound to you, my friend?" sheriff Talley said, smiling like she had hope for a good outcome. "I can't promise you anything, but I can promise we will do our best to find out exactly what happened."

"And I already told Nancy I'm helping," Terry bellowed out. "I don't have nothin' so pressing that I can't help my old buddy find his bride."

"I don't know what I'd do without you guys. I don't know how to thank you. And I'm sorry you had to make such a fuss over me," Elijah said in the most heartfelt way. "I'm not worthy of anybody fussing over me."

Terry stepped closer to the bed and opened the bible, "You can thank me by leaning on God. That's the only thing that's going to get us through this. I can tell you, without a doubt, she would want you to. Read his word and then listen for him to guide you. If you don't listen, you might miss directions."

Elijah began to flip through the pages, and it landed on one. It was in the book of Jeremiah. In the middle of that page, was a bookmark with a scripture on it. It was Jeremiah verse twenty-nine verse eleven and it read *"I know the plans I have for you, declares the Lord; plans to prosper you and not to harm you, plans to give you hope and a future."*

"There couldn't be a more perfect scripture for this moment," Ella spoke gently, leaning over Elijah, resting her cheek against his. "Mama knew what message she wanted to give, and I think she gave it perfectly."

"Geneva," Elijah whispered softly. "Where are you?"

"Eli," Terry said. "Do what the doctors say, and I mean everything they say, and leave this to us, at least until you feel better. You know I'm not a quitter and besides, miss Geneva still owes me a dance."

"What?" Elijah said, Terry, pulling him out of the melancholy mood for the moment. "What are you talking about?"

"Don't you remember when Sherry and I saw you two out at the dance hall one night about six months ago," Terry continued.

"Vaguely," Elijah countered.

"Well, Geneva kept telling me she was saving me a dance, but everybody kept grabbing her," Terry said. "I swear she had more get up and go than the youngsters out there."

"Oh, yes," Elijah nodded. "I remember now. She wasn't happy I wouldn't dance, but you know I have two left feet, Terry."

"And when you two left, she turned back to me and said, *you get the first dance next time Terry and that's a promise*, and I'm holding her to it," he said comically.

"I'll tell her when I see her," Elijah smiled, trying to be as confident as he could about her being okay, but deep down, a different feeling lingered, trying its best to fill any positive thoughts.

After a few minutes of talking, in walked a nurse, taking vital signs and asking some questions on what happened. Everyone left the room, waiting in the hall until they were finished the testing, they needed to make sure his heart was okay. Then a doctor walked in. He wasn't very tall, a bit of a heavy built, with salt and pepper hair.

"I'm Dr. Byron," he said, looking over the tests the nurses had run. "It looks like you just had a pretty bad anxiety attack. Do you have a lot going on right now that might cause that?"

"You might say that doc," Elijah answered, looking at Ella and Caleb as they re-entered the room. "This is my daughter Ella and her husband Caleb."

"Nice to meet you," the doctor said, extending his hand out to them. "Anything you can do to keep your father calm and as stress-free as possible, would really help. Anxiety attacks can be very harmful, so just keep an eye on him. In the meantime, I'm prescribing him some medication to help him. Do you have any questions for me?"

"Can my dad go home," Ella asked, looking over at Elijah, hoping the answer was yes.

"I don't see why not," the doctor answered, once more looking down at his clipboard and notes. "Is there anyone who can stay with him?"

"We will doctor," Ella said, grabbing Caleb's hand.

"We will too," Jimmy said, his foursome following behind.

"I thought you had to get back home?" Elijah asked, not unhappy about it.

"Awww, things can wait," Jimmy said. "Right guys?"

"Absolutely," Brenda said, going over to Elijah and holding his hand. "We got each other. That's how it's supposed to be right?"

"Right sis?" he replied, smiling knowing his house would still be filled with laughter. "Besides, I haven't heard all of Jim's stories. I know he has more. Don't ya Jim?"

"You got it, brother-in-law," Jimmy answered, flashing those baby blues, and grinning like he couldn't wait to start.

"Remember," the doctor said. "Keep calm, get plenty of rest and eat right. If you have any more problems, come back to see us. Hopefully, you won't need to."

"I'll be fine doc," Elijah said, looking around the room. "I think I'm in good hands."

Nodding, "I'll have them come back with your discharge papers. Take care, Mr. James."

Elijah listened to that crazy bunch he called family, carry on, He was more than ready to get out of that room with white walls, a bed like a brick, and sheets you could see through, not to mention the smell all hospitals expelled from the first whiff. He was just ready to be in his own bed, covered up with the quilt that held such memories. He wanted to be in his own house where it all started and hopefully, where it would continue.

"Here you go Mr. James," the nurse said, handing him a few papers to sign. "I hope you feel better."

"I already do," he answered, signing what she asked, then shewing everyone out of the room so he could get dressed.

"You need me to help Pop?" Caleb asked, an unusual request on a normal day, but right then, it was a good idea.

Once he was ready, they pulled the car around and wheeled him to the back exit. Elijah didn't want to be pushed in a wheelchair because he said he wasn't old, but that's all it took for Jimmy to start in on him. He listened to Jimmy until they could get him situated in the car and finally on their way home.

"You really okay dad?" Ella said. "I mean really. You scared me so much."

"I just got a little…"

"Overwhelmed, I figured that. But you have to stay calm like the doctor said," she added. "We don't want to worry like that again."

"I'll do my best Ella. I promise," Elijah smiled.

Happily making it home and getting into bed, everyone else went downstairs and did their best to be as quiet as possible, although it was hard for a few of them. But with Elijah's door shut, it muffled most of the sounds from downstairs easily. He remembered what Terry told him. And after getting ready for bed and climbing under the multicolored quilt, he picked up the bible Geneva never got a chance to give to him. Elijah held it close to his heart for a moment, then he opened it, not sure where to start. He began to fan the pages, hoping something would tell him where to stop, and strangely enough, it did. The first time when Terry did that, it stopped on the bookmark, but when Elijah did the same, it stopped again. There was a small, folded note buried in the creases.

CHAPTER SEVENTEEN

The small note, simply read, "God loves you and so do I...
Geneva..." Her handwriting was, without a doubt, recognizable the way she swirled her S and swooped her Y. It said nothing else, but in one short sentence, she said a world's worth, instilling in him a sense of peace and hope. For some reason, Elijah got a feeling such a small gesture, was a sign from God. Something told him to never give up on finding her.

"I won't give up God," Elijah said out loud, with eyes closed and heart open. "I'll never give up."

"Pop," Caleb said, quietly knocking, then opening his door. "Who were you talking to?"

"Nobody," Elijah quickly replied, then changed his answer. "I was talking to God. I figured it was about time I did, don't you think?"

Smiling back, Caleb said, "I just wanted to say good night."

"And checking on me?" Elijah smiled back. "I know you were checking on me."

"Well," Caleb replied honestly. "I was voted to be the one to come up to make sure you were okay. Jimmy wanted to, but we figured you'd never get any sleep if he did."

"I'm okay, really," Elijah answered. "You guys enjoy your time together. And if I can't sleep, I may come down to join you. I am pretty tired though."

"Just rest Pop and we'll see you in the morning. If you need anything, just holler. Everything will be okay," he said, giving a quick nod and leaving.

Elijah heard Caleb's footsteps tread downstairs, leaving him with a good feeling inside. With everything going on, peace filled him completely.

How can this be Lord, he spoke aloud? *How can I not be upset and worried? I don't understand.*

With such thoughts roaming around in his head, he found a perfect and comfortable spot in his bed, one he didn't want to move from. Elijah pulled the covers up around his neck and let out a long sigh. *Goodnight, Geneva,* he muttered to himself, with many hopes his dreams would carry him, once again, to her. Since so many memories of their past were in the forefront of his mind, he figured it just might. And God must've been listening.

Elijah opened his eyes, thinking it was morning. It was, but morning at a different time. He was still covered up by that old quilt and everything else was the same, but then…

"If you're a gonna take me on that picnic you promised, you best get your tail outa bed. I swear Elijah, I didn't think you'd ever wake up. I fixed breakfast and left a few home-made biscuits for ya to munch on before we leave," Geneva said, wheeling around grabbing this and that. "Besides, Ella and Caleb are meetin' us. Don't you remember?"

"Caleb?" Elijah asked, still in a state of confusion.

"You know, our new son-in-law," she said, standing over him like she was about to yank him up herself. "What in Heaven's name is wrong with you? We don't see'em much and a day out in nature is just what the doctor ordered."

"Yes ma'am," Elijah replied. "I'm getting up now. It won't take me long."

"You got fifteen minutes," she said, walking toward the bedroom door. "I'll have the baskets ready then. Don't you make me wait."

Elijah knew she meant what she said, and rubbed the sleep from his eyes, swung around, and put his feet on the floor. Never really being an early riser except when he had to earlier in life, it always took a minute to get his wits about him to function properly.

"Ten minutes," Geneva yelled from downstairs. "Shake your tail feathers Elijah."

He laughed to himself, hearing her voice ring loud and clear, "Coming," Elijah yelled back.

Finally making his way downstairs, comb in hand, still grooming himself as he walked, Geneva stood by the front door with two picnic baskets, one on each side.

"We feeding an army?" Elijah laughed

"Honey, you know how Caleb likes to eat, but I swear it don't show a bit. Wish I could do that," she said. "And sometimes you get your fill too Elijah James."

"I do like fried chicken, and I think that's what I smell," he replied, holding his nose up in the air taking a whiff. "Yep, it's fried chicken."

Geneva hit Elijah on the arm playfully, "You rascal, just grab them there keys and let's go. They're meetin' us at lake Wright Patman shortly."

"Should I grab the poles," Elijah said, a sparkle showing in his eyes.

"We'll go fishin' another day," she said, motioning with her head to get going.

Still trying to completely wake up, he quickly grabbed a homemade biscuit from the kitchen table and caught up with her. Her little legs went faster than a chicken when it's being chased. Her age sure didn't show in her actions in the least.

They got the car loaded and headed toward the lake and Geneva sat there admiring the beautiful colors of fall. Her eyes lit up with every shade of red or orange, entwined with a few shades of green the trees left behind. It's something she always did. It was like a ritual to her.

"Boy, God sure outdone himself," Geneva said, still peering out. "Ain't it beautiful Elijah? Only God could've put somethin' together so perfectly."

Only listening, but not answering her, mostly because she didn't really expect an answer. She just liked to talk about God. It seemed like the more Elijah ignored such conversations, the more she spoke about a higher power.

It wasn't long and they pulled up to the spot they agreed to meet, and Ella and Caleb were throwing down a huge blanket on the ground with an ice chest sitting next to it. Geneva looked at the two newlyweds, and got emotional, helping get the baskets out of the car.

"Why do you look like you're going to cry, Geneva?" Elijah asked, shaking his head, never understanding women in the least.

"It feels like yesterday when we brought that little girl into the world, Elijah. Times a passin' too quick I tell ya," she answered, holding back her emotions best she could.

"But look at her," Elijah said, putting his arm around Geneva and pulling her close. "She's talented, beautiful, and caring, just like you."

"Oh," Geneva said. "Sometimes you can be a sweet one can't ya? Come on let's get them vittles over there before Caleb passes out."

The vision of that moment was as clear as bell, Elijah reliving a moment that wasn't significant at the time, but more special the more he thought. It wasn't long, something unexpected would force him to leave such a time once again.

"Hey Pop," Caleb called out, then Elijah opened his eyes to see him standing over him. "I swear you get harder and harder to wake up each day. Sometimes I wonder if you're even going to."

Letting out a frustrated breath, "Sometimes I wish I could stay asleep," Elijah replied, sitting up. "What time is it?"

"It's around nine o'clock. You sleep well? I checked on you a few times and you were smiling in your sleep," Caleb grinned. "You ready for breakfast?"

"Sounds good," Elijah said, patting Caleb on the arm. "And...uh, I had a lot to smile about."

Elijah went downstairs to find everyone chowing down on pancakes and sausage, and there was just enough left to make one more good plate, so he did just that. Ella wasn't talking much, and it drew a red flag immediately. She always gave an energetic good morning, but not then. The sun's rays showed through the window spotlighting his one and only daughter, her blonde hair shimmering, but she wasn't her usual perky self.

"Okay," Elijah asked, looking in Ella's direction. "What's going on?"

"What do you mean dad?" Ella said, trying to dodge the question by continuing to wash dishes, banging a few plates around in the process, to make noise.

"I won't take another bite until you tell me," Elijah continued. "And you know I don't bluff."

She stopped washing dishes, dried her hands, and turned to him. The look on her face was confusing. It wasn't happy or sad, but somewhere smack dab in the middle. Her eyes were normally easy to read, but for once, they weren't.

"Dad," Ella said. "Sheriff Talley came by this morning."

"To check on me?" Elijah said, putting another bite in his mouth. "They are real gems you know. Good people."

"Well, yes, he wanted to make sure you were okay, but he...also...he wanted a picture of mama," she said hesitantly, afraid it would upset him. "He's going to make up posters around the Shreveport area and see if anyone comes forward with information."

"That's good right?" he nodded, "That's what we want them to do. They're doing their job Ella, that's all."

"You're right," she responded quickly, her mood livening up after. "It's a positive thing. It's the first step in..."

"Finding my Geneva," Elijah said, finishing Ella's sentence perfectly, then turning to Jimmy, Brenda, Tom, and Bridget. "I thought you were leaving yesterday."

"Don't you remember brother?" Brenda said. "We told you we weren't leaving just yet. We want to be here with you until you find out something. Besides, Jimmy is getting pretty fond of this place."

"Don't get too comfortable, "Elijah picked, then laughed after.

After eating, Tom asked Elijah if he would like to talk a walk. Knowing he hadn't really spent much time with his brother-in-law, Elijah grabbed a jacket, and they left the others in the living room, chatting and trying to agree on what show to watch.

The cool breeze whisked by, making every tree around look like they were dancing. When they made it to the spot where you could see everything, they stopped. There were a few big boulders, good enough to make a seat out of, and so they did. For a few moments, Elijah found comfort in such a view, just like Geneva always did. Strange, but she taught him many things even if he wasn't aware of it.

"Elijah," Tom said softly. "I know you're worried and I know you don't want to let it show. But sometimes you have to lean on the people who love you. That's why we're staying. We love you."

"I don't quite know what to say Tom," Elijah muttered, the whistling wind playing its song. "We've never really been close, but...I'd like to be. I think I always let the worst part

of me show, like a shield to guard against getting hurt, but…
what I didn't know. I was hurting myself."

"I understand," Tom nodded, lowering his head. "I think
everybody's done that. There's no shame in admitting it and
going forward as a different, but better person."

Once more looking out into the distance, the hills swal-
lowing up the land with their beauty, and Tom could tell his
thoughts were miles from where they stood.

"What's on your mind Elijah?" Tom asked kindly. "Geneva, I know."

"We used to come up here all the time. Geneva would
make up some sandwiches and lemonade, and we would sit
on this ground like we were somewhere famous just enjoying the view," Elijah smiled, still looking out.

"Sounds nice," Tom smiled, glancing in the same direction, taking in the sight.

About then, they heard, "Hey," Jimmy yelled out. "Come
back to the house."

"Why?" Tom asked, in a louder voice than anyone ever
heard from him before.

"Just come back. We have some news," Jimmy answered,
going back into the house.

CHAPTER EIGHTEEN

Tom and Elijah hurried the best they could, trying not to stumble on the way down to the house, and Tom held onto Elijah's arm for support. Everyone came out on the front porch as they made it to the steps. Bundled up in their jackets, Ella locked the front door.

"Wait a minute," Elijah said. "What's happening?"

"Terry said he might have some news," Bridget answered before anyone else had a chance. "He sounded pretty confident brother, and you know Terry."

"Did he say what he found?" Elijah asked, his curiosity and excitement getting the best of him.

"I guess we'll find out Pop," Caleb said, treading toward the car.

Without another question asked, they went in the direction of Terry's bail bond business across the street from the sheriff's office. It was in a somewhat deteriorating part of town, but it didn't affect Terry. People needed him no matter where he was located.

They passed by an apartment complex on the right, and the turn was ahead. It seemed like everything in Elijah dropped to his stomach, his nerves getting the best of him. He didn't know if the news was something he didn't want to hear or the kind of news that would give him hope. Sitting in the back seat, Elijah's mind went in every direction it could possibly go. A part of him said Geneva was with Terry waiting to give him a big hug, but then another voice told him that was crazy thinking. Nonetheless, his heart was racing, and he had to do all he could to breathe slowly and calm down as the paramedic told him. He couldn't afford to go back to the hospital.

When they pulled up and got out, Terry was standing inside, looking through the glass front door. Moving aside as they went in, Jimmy and the others pulled in. He motioned for them to go into his office down the hall. When everyone was inside, he finally started to talk.

"Well," Terry said, thumbing through some papers on his desk. "I took pictures of those receipts in Geneva's car and where she was that day she disappeared, so I took it upon myself to make a few calls."

"And.." Elijah said, on the edge of his seat, literally, waiting for him to continue.

"I talked to a lady who remembered Geneva. She remembered her buying those things we found in her car, especially the bible. In fact, she's the one who sold them to her," Terry said.

"Where was it?" Ella asked, not sure how to feel with such news.

"It was a place off Youree Drive, some Christian store with gifts and so forth," Terry answered. "It's called Faith Alley, Books & Gifts. It's only been open a year or so, maybe."

Elijah muttered aloud, "She always brought up wanting to go there and maybe…"

"That's where she wanted you to take her that day dad… that's it," Ella said, finishing his thought.

"Anyway," Terry added. "I told her we would try to make a trip up that way today if you folks want to. Then we can talk to her face to face and get every bit of information we can. I already talked to the sheriff, and she said to report back what we find."

"Why don't you, Ella and Caleb go," Jimmy said to Elijah. "The rest of us will go back to your place and get a few things caught up in your yard and shop so you don't have to worry about it. But call us the minute you know something."

Elijah gave a nod and patted Jimmy on the shoulder, and they went back home. It's like the room was spinning for Elijah, sitting down reflecting on the last moment he saw Geneva. She was sitting in the living room writing with her bible in her lap. Then, he went to the one person he knew could hear him even if he wasn't talking aloud, God. He closed his eyes, *Dear God, I know I don't have the right to ask you for help after all the years I ignored you, but we need your help now. Please help us find Geneva. God, I know if she's with you, she's in a grand place, but if she's not, please guide us to her. I will listen to you. I never have in the past, but I promise I will now.*

Elijah could feel a hand resting on his shoulder, his eyes opened to find Ella standing next to him smiling, "Dad, you ready to go?"

"I've been ready," he answered with enthusiasm and energy. "I didn't run after her when I should've, but I'm going to make up for it now."

"We gonna stand around here and talk all day long or are we gonna be private eyes and find this young lady," Terry said, wearing the unmistakable grin that only he could pull off. "Let's go, Eli."

Elijah snapped out of the thoughts in his head bringing him back to reality, and they all climbed into Terry's truck. Ella opted to get in the back because she knew how two friends like to talk, so she gave them that chance. And knowing there was an hour drive ahead, she rested her head back to take a quick nap before they were to begin such a search.

"You got a great girl back there," Terry smiled, glancing slightly back to Ella. "You did a great job with her."

Elijah gave a short chuckle, "To be honest Terry, I didn't do it. Everything Ella is Geneva put in her. She gave her a kind spirit, loving nature, and faith in God. None of that came from me," Elijah said honestly, lowering his head when he was finished.

"Don't cut yourself short Eli. I've known you for a long, long time my friend and I always knew there was something special in you. Geneva knew it too," he said, then laughed a little. "That's why she put up with you for so many years."

"Very funny," Elijah said, cutting his eyes over to Terry. "But maybe you're right. It took me a long time, but I finally found God."

Elijah could tell Terry started getting emotional by the change in his expression instantly, "When Elijah. When did you find God?"

"We went to that cowboy church Geneva always attended and somehow brother Todd got to me, and I couldn't push it away," Elijah said. "I don't understand it."

"God got to you through brother Todd," Terry explained. "It was your time to finally see clearly. Maybe it took that long for a reason. None of us know God's reason for anything, but we have to trust in his plan."

"I should've hung out with you more when we were younger and maybe…" Elijah started to say.

"It's his plan. It wasn't meant for us to hang out so much then, but he has us together now for a reason," Terry said, reaching over and nudging Elijah.

"No more looking back," Elijah said.

"No more looking back Eli," Terry repeated Elijah. "Let's just look forward to, hopefully finding this crazy, energetic, straightforward, and faith-filled lady we all know and love. What do you say?"

With a solid nod, then looking straight ahead at the road, a burst of positivity ran through every inch of Elijah's body.

It was a feeling of thinking everything would be okay until there was a reason to think otherwise. Elijah remembered a scripture Geneva used to read to him. She never thought he heard it, but he did, and it was one he remembered because it made sense. It was in Matthew and said *Therefore do not worry about tomorrow, for tomorrow will worry about itself. Each day has enough trouble of its own.* As the words of that scripture massaged his mind, he allowed it to soak in, letting whatever worries he had, drift far away, leaving only good thoughts.

Almost in a trans-like state, Elijah's eyes were fixed on the road, not much on either side to gain his attention. The road, somehow had a hypnotizing quality, watching the lines in the middle quickly come and go, calming him by the minute. Somehow, his heartbeats were no longer racing, but slow and steady.

"Not much further," Terry said, turning to Elijah then back to the road. "Maybe another ten miles."

Still relaxed and enjoying the ride, Elijah looked back to see Ella resting peacefully, her head leaning up against the window. He knew she had to be exhausted, mentally, and emotionally through everything happening, but it never showed. It's like she was doing her best to take care of him when she needed to be taken care of too. In a way, a little guilt wiggled its way into Elijah's mind. It was telling him he only thought of himself and didn't care about anyone else, but he also knew it was evil speaking, not God. For the first time, he could tell the difference between good and evil, and it felt good.

They pulled into Shreveport and passed convenient stores on the left and right, then a shopping center just before reaching the highway. Terry drove further down, following the directions to the Christian store. Going through the downtown area, people were everywhere. Most were probably finding their way to one of the casinos, but some appeared to be homeless or just wandering around. Flashing lights in the windows of almost every place they looked, showed what the night life probably was like.

It didn't take long to get there. Terry pulled in and parked. It sat amid a cluster of different shops aligned on both sides of the road. From candle and Scentsy to souvenir shops, clothing stores and everything in between, there was a little stretch of places Elijah knew Geneva probably loved.

"Ella honey," Elijah said, reaching in the back seat. "We're here."

Ella Stretched and moaned a little, waking up from her short-lived nap, and let out a long, *I'm awake*, sigh. It was obvious she needed the rest, but once she realized they were at one of the last places her mama was seen, she woke up quickly. Gathering her purse and putting on her jacket, Terry, being a gentleman, opened her door and helped her out.

"Why, thank you sir," she said kindly to Terry, shutting the door when she was out. "I thought chivalry was dead."

"Not until I'm gone ma'am," Terry replied kindly.

"I bet you spoil Sherry to death," Ella said, stopping and turning to him.

"I sure try," Terry replied. "I figure I was blessed with her, then I need to take care of her best I can. Besides, she's worth it."

The three of them stepped closer to the front door of the store, noticing the many details it portrayed. The store window displayed the most beautiful pictures and plaques with inspirational sayings to unique crosses, big and small. There were quilts with the word *faith* on them and personalized picture albums in all colors. Going inside, the first thing Elijah saw, was a few tables of bibles. Some big, some small, some with large print and others with print tiny enough you could barely read. There was something for everyone. They even had bibles dedicated for boys and for girls with devotionals built right into them. It was no wonder Geneva wanted to come to such a place.

Then Elijah saw something, walking closer to it, he reached over and picked up the very bible Geneva had bought for him. He opened it, but this time, there weren't any notes to stop it at any page, but still beautiful.

"Can I help you sir?" a lady's voice said.

Elijah turned to see a lady with medium length blondish hair, dressed in jeans and boots, and her dark eyes reflected a confident boldness. With her arms in front of her and fingers laced together, she showed nothing but a smile.

"Ma'am," Terry cut in. "I'm the one you talked to about Miss Geneva, the lady we're looking for."

"Oh yes," she said, walking back toward the counter. "I remember her well."

"What was it that made you remember her? I'm sure you get lots of customers in the quaint little store," Ella asked.

The lady chuckled before she spoke, "I'll tell you something. I have never met anyone more unforgettable. She had me laughing the entire time she was here. I bet she shopped around for more than an hour. She picked up everything in this place, lookin' at and reading everything. I fell in love with her candidness and country talk."

"She's a straightforward one for sure," Elijah replied with a grin.

"But what I loved the most," the woman said. "Was her faith. I could feel it all around her. And when she asked for me to help her find a bible for her husband who didn't have much faith at, I was more than happy to do so. I'm all about helping people find the right path. And I could tell she was too."

"I'm her husband," Elijah hesitantly muttered. "And we found the bible in her car. It's beautiful."

"She was hoping you'd like it, and we prayed over it before she left," the woman said. "We prayed for God to take your anger and replace it with joy, to heal your spirit and fill it with love."

"You prayed over it? You prayed for me?" Elijah responded, surprised.

"We sure did. Your wife said, *if that there man don't find the Lord with this, he's gonna get a whippin' from me and from God.* I remember that like it was yesterday."

"Sounds just like her," Terry laughed. "You sounded just like her."

"Well, I am a might country myself. By the way, my name is Kimber Moore. My husband Mark pastors a cowboy church in these parts. And this store has been a blessing to us from the people we meet here…including your wife."

By that time, Terry was positive she knew exactly who they were looking for and tried his best to see if there was any information to help them find the direction she may have headed when leaving that store.

"Do you know where she was going when she left here?" Terry asked, notepad and pen ready to jot everything down.

"Let me see," she replied, sitting down, and placing her elbow on the counter, in a thinking position. "She said something about going a few stores down on the other side of the alleyway."

"Did you see her go that way?" Terry continued to question.

"She pulled her van down in front of the other store, but in a few minutes when I looked again, it was gone," she answered. "I thought it was kind of strange, but I didn't think any more about it. I just figured she changed her mind and left."

"Which store was it," Ella jumped in, somewhat anxious to dig deeper into what happened to her mama.

"I told her Scentsy Surprise Inc. on the next block, had some really great smelling candles, oils, and such. She said she loved to make her place smell good, and I just assumed that's where she went."

"Right past the alley?" Terry said, writing down everything said.

"Yes sir," Kimber replied.

"Thank you for your time," Terry said, starting for the door.

"Elijah," Kimber called out just before they left.

"How did you know my name?" Elijah asked.

"Like I said, we talked a lot and I'm the one who put your name on the bible. I didn't forget such a name. And I wanted to tell you," She said, coming closer and putting her hand over his. "She sure does love you. The way she talked about you; it was evident. Even if you don't find her, know that. But also know God is with her wherever she is."

"Thank you," Elijah smiled, a tear finding a path down his cheek. "You don't know how much I needed that."

They nodded to each other, and appreciation for the moment floated around them, truly inspiring. They said their goodbyes and walked down the block. The sign Kimber told them about was just down the way. There was a small table and a couple of chairs sitting just outside the door with a few samples on it. Opening the door, a bell went off.

"Be right out," a voice called out.

Ella, being a woman, regardless of the reason for being there, roamed around the store, smelling everything in sight, picking one big red candle up in the process. Then a young girl came out. She couldn't have been any more than nineteen years old but carried herself in a more mature manner.

"This might be a crazy question," Terry said. "But we're looking for a woman who might have been in here about six weeks ago. Around this area is the last place we know she was. Here's her picture."

"Ummm," the girl started. "I think it might've been her, but she never came inside."

"What do you mean? Then how do you know it was her?" Terry continued.

"She started to open the door and I spoke to her, but then a man came up to her and she shut it back," the girl explained.

"Do you remember anything about the man?" Terry asked, getting more information than he thought he would.

"Just that he looked like he might've been trying to bum money from her. It concerned me, so I watched for a minute until the phone rang and I had to answer it. When I looked back, her vehicle was gone, so I figured she was too."

"What happened to the man?" Terry asked.

"He was gone too," she answered. "Is she okay?"

"We hope so," Terry replied. "Thank you for your help."

"Wait," she said, handing him a piece of paper and a pen. "Write your name and number down and if I hear of anything else, I'll give you a call."

He did as she asked, putting his number, the sheriff's, and Elijah's down just in case she or anyone else knew anything. He handed it to her, and she put it under the register drawer.

When Terry walked out, he had a very bewildered look across his face, peering left then right, like he was trying to make the pieces fit.

"The Alley," Terry said, looking between the two buildings. Then he went off on his own past the big dumpster about a quarter of the way down.

Elijah and Ella followed a few steps behind until Terry stopped. On the other side of the dumpster was a tarp looking piece of material laid across something or someone. No movement was seen under it and Terry took a deep breath.

"Move back Eli," he told Elijah and Ella, giving hand motions. "Get back."

"What?" Elijah said.

Then Terry slowly, but carefully grabbed the top corner of the tarp and started lifting it.

CHAPTER NINETEEN

"**W**hat are you doing?" a man hollered out. "This keeps me warm. Go away."

Terry let out a breath, relieved he didn't find what he thought he might, instead, he found a homeless man. His clothes were torn and tattered, and he had on an old faded green army jacket that wouldn't even come close to keeping him warm. The beard covering his wrinkled skin looked like it hadn't been combed in months and they could tell he hadn't eaten in some time.

"I'm sorry," Terry apologized, starting to cover him back up, then stopping as he Noticed a little diner across the street. He looked back at the man, "Are you hungry? Would you let me buy you some lunch?"

"I don't even know your name," the man said in a grouchy tone.

"The name is Terry," he said kindly. "What's your name, sir?

A little hesitant, looking around first, then "It's Benjamin," he said, wiping his face. "Benjamin Weathers. My friends always called me Bennie, but I don't have many folks left now. The ones I do, don't care if I'm alive or dead."

"Well Bennie, are you hungry," Terry asked once more, Elijah and Ella looking on, watching Terry's kindness spread all around in that grim alley.

"I suppose I could eat," Bennie said. "But I can't pay ya back I want you to know. I…"

"I don't want to be paid back, Bennie. I just want to get you something to eat. Let me help you up," Terry said, extending his hand and lifting the man to his feet. "These are my friends Eli and Ella."

"Glad to meet you, folks," he said, nodding and following alongside Terry as they made their way to the diner just across from where they were.

Just a hop skip and jump, they walked up to the small restaurant and went in. All the tables were covered with red and white checked vinyl tablecloths and the small bar in front of the kitchen was surrounded by swivel stools. The one waitress working, went to the few in the place, taking their orders. The look she gave, was nothing short of judgmental, but it didn't matter. They found a table in the corner and sat down. Bennie took the corner seat against the wall and watched the others as they joined him.

"What'll ya have?" the waitress asked, staring at Bennie the entire time.

"Coffee please," Bennie said, glancing at Terry to make sure it was okay. "And maybe a burger and fries."

Elijah, Terry, and Ella decided on the same looking at a less than desirable menu they offered, and the waitress walked away, still glancing back.

"People don't understand," Bennie said, his hands shaking as he spoke. "I never wanted to be like this."

"What's your story?" Terry asked. "I'd like to know. Everybody's got a story."

"Well sir, I was in the Army for over twenty years. I've seen things no one should ever see and experienced things no one should ever experience. It takes a toll on a person ya know?" he started. "When I got out, something inside me was different. It's like I lost myself in the wars and battles, shootings, and deaths before my eyes. I lost those I considered friends more times than I want to count...but nobody understood."

"I understand," Elijah replied in a sympathetic tone. "I was never in the war, but I knew people who were, and they told me similar stories. It's tough."

"Anyway, I never could get it together. I finally ended up losing everyone I cared about because of these demons in my mind, constantly haunting me. So here I am homeless, wondering why God would allow it. Why doesn't he help? I used to talk to him and even had a bible, but it was gone one morning when I woke up."

"Is this where you live, or do you go different places?" Terry asked, handing him the cup of coffee when she came back to the table.

"Mostly I'm here. The dumpster and buildings block the wind for the most part and on cold nights I just pray for warmth," he said sipping slowly. "You folks from around here?"

"We're trying to find a friend," Terry answered. "We're from Texarkana."

"My wife." Elijah said. "Her name's Geneva and this is the last place anyone saw her before she disappeared."

"I'm sorry to hear that," Bennie said. "How long has she been missing?"

About that time the waitress came over with their meals. Bennie tore into his burger like he hadn't seen food in quite some time, but still paying attention to Elijah.

"About six weeks or so," Elijah said. "The lady at the Christian store told us she saw her park in front of the candle place, but then was gone."

"Six weeks," Bennie muttered, still eating. "What color was her car?"

"It was a red van," Elijah said. "And the young girl in the other store said she saw some man talking to Geneva, so she never went into the store. Then she was gone."

"Hmmm," he sounded off. "There was a disturbance in the alley one day, but like I said, I cover up so no one knows I'm there."

"Disturbance," Terry jumped in. "What kind of disturbance?"

"Well, there was this guy I ain't ever seen before roaming up and down the alley one day, about that long ago. Everyone who parked down this road, he'd ask them for money. Most folks were with other people, so he left them alone." he said. "He kept talking to himself like he was on something, but who am I to judge. My memory's not so great these days, but if I think of anything else, I can let you know. Write your number down."

"I'd appreciate that," Terry said, everyone finishing their meals. "And if you need anything as well, give me a call."

"I don't need anything, but that's kind. I been makin' it all this time, I suppose I'll keep on makin' it just fine," Bennie smiled, appreciation painted across his face.

"All you have to do is call," Terry said, getting up to pay the ticket, leaving a tip even though the lady wasn't the kindest person he'd ever met. "Hey Bennie, before we leave, I want you to take a little walk with us."

"Where to?" Bennie asked in a curious way.

Bennie followed them back across the street to the first store they went into, the Christian store. Kimber was walking around straightening things up and turned to see them when they walked back in.

"Did you find anything out?" she asked like she was genuinely concerned. "I've been thinkin' about you guys ever since you left."

"No ma'am, but I would like to buy a bible and get it engraved," Terry said, patting Bennie on the back. "Go pick one out...anyone you like and a cover too."

"I couldn't sir...I..."

Terry interrupted, "It's a gift. Now don't take a blessing away from me by not accepting a gift."

Not saying a word, Bennie started crying, his tears cleaning some of the dirt from his face as he wiped them away. It's like the emotions he'd been holding in for a long time, finally made their way to the surface and all it took was kindness from someone he didn't know.

"I'm not mad at God," Bennie said. "I think I'm just mad at myself for my own choices and actions. Sometimes it just seems easier to blame God than myself."

Elijah stepped up and stood in front of Bennie as he tried his best to compose himself, "I understand. I was a mean ole buzzard, as my wife would've put it, for a long time. I didn't even give God a second thought, but not any-more. Believe and things will get better. Whether I find my Geneva or not, she saved me with her faith. Maybe we can do the same for you."

Bennie went to one of the first tables and there sat the exact bible Geneva had bought Elijah, "Can I have this one?"

"Absolutely," Terry said. "How do you want her to en-grave it?"

"Bennie Weathers…because you folks are my friends," he said, handing the bible over to Kimber.

"Do you have a picture of Geneva?" Bennie asked sin-cerely.

Terry pulled one from his wallet and handed it to Ben-nie, "This is her."

"Beautiful lady…and those eyes, so blue," Bennie smiled. "Can I keep it?"

Bennie gave a nod and it wasn't long before Kimber came back out with the bible he picked out. On her way to him, she stopped and picked up a bible cover that would weather the elements and a few bookmarks as well.

"Here ya go Mr. Weathers," Kimber said, with a smile that could light up the darkest place.

"Call me Bennie," he said. "My friends call me Bennie."

"How much do I owe you?" Terry asked, pulling out his wallet.

"It's on the house," Kimber replied kindly.

"No…no, I'm gonna pay you for it," Terry insisted.

"Now don't take a blessing away from me by not accepting a gift," she replied in a sly way.

Bennie stared at the both of them and began to smile bigger than he had in a very long time, "What in the world did I do to deserve such beautiful people doing such wonderful things for me? You folks are angels," Bennie said, going over and hugging everyone, one at a time, sharing the joy placed in his heart. "I'll never forget this. I'll never forget this day."

"Where do you live Bennie?" Kimber asked.

Lowering his head, shame showing, "In the Alley, past the dumpster. I have nowhere else to go, but I'm okay."

Instantly, tears began to form in Kimber's eyes like a waterfall of emotion overtaking her. The kind of person she was, showed without a word spoken. Then she turned, picked up her phone and dialed a number.

"Mark," she said sweetly. "We're gonna have a guest stay with us for a bit. Is that okay?"

Unable to hear what he said, but her smile said it all. "It's settled," she said, wiping the moisture from her eyes. "We want you to come stay with us. We'd be honored if you would." She told Bennie.

"But I couldn't…I"

"Don't be stealing a blessing from her Bennie," Ella interrupted, smiling the entire time.

"That's right," Kimber said. "Now, go get what you have and bring them right over. You can help me around here until close and we may even go shopping to get you some new duds. How does that sound?"

No words came, but Bennie leaned over and hugged her like he'd known her his entire life. The expression on his face showed a glimpse of hope, something he thought he lost a long time ago.

Terry wasn't only smiling outwardly, but inside as well. And Elijah looked on and took in what just happened. It was like a miracle before his eyes. They were out trying to save Geneva but ended up playing a part in saving someone else's life instead.

"I guess we better be going," Elijah said. "Thank you for trying to help."

"If we hear anything, we'll give you a call, right Bennie."

"Right," Bennie replied, grinning from ear to ear like he'd been given a new lease on life and a chance to live again.

"But remember," Kimber said. "God brought you here for a reason. This is a journey you're supposed to take. Enjoy it, treasure it and embrace it. I pray for you all."

Elijah, Ella, and Terry said their goodbyes and headed back to the car. Elijah's thoughts took over, trying to figure out what really happened there. Then thinking about what Kimber said about the journey. Something told him, she was right.

They got in the car and started back home, and Elijah did as before, looking around, trying his best not to worry. Ella wasn't saying a word either. It's like all three of them were trying to process such an experience.

"Where do we go from here?" Elijah said aloud, not really talking to anyone. "What do we do now?"

"We did a good thing Eli," Terry said. "We helped someone who desperately needed it. If we hadn't come to look for Geneva, we'd a never found him to start with. It's like the old saying *'Everything happens for a reason.'* I think we were supposed to be here on this day in that place."

"Maybe," Elijah replied. "It did feel good to help someone."

"I've never heard you say anything like that dad," Ella chimed in. "It's good to hear. And it did warm my heart. It makes you think about how many people need help that no one knows about."

"I know about your mama," Elijah said. "She needs help."

Ella leaned forward to the front, "I believe we're going to find her dad. I have to believe it. And today was just a start…the start to following his path to her."

The ride back to Texarkana was a quiet one for the most part. Terry had the radio on an old country station, and he sang along with it when he knew the words. So much went on, no one thought to call Jimmy to let them know what happened, then again, there wasn't much to tell. And after almost an hour of driving, Terry pulled back up to his office and parked.

"I'm sorry we didn't find out more Eli," Terry said, shaking his head. "But we have a starting point."

"It's not your fault Terry," Elijah replied.

"Thank you for wanting to help," Ella added.

"You guys know me and I'm not a quitter. I have a few ideas and will call you if I find out anything else. That's a promise," Terry said, getting out and opening Ella's door.

"Still the gentleman," Ella smiled.

"You guys go home and try not to worry, especially you Eli. Take care of yourself and don't land yourself back in that hospital. But if you do, I'll be there," Terry said, shaking his hand as they left.

Ella and Elijah went home and told the rest what happened and how incredible of an experience it was. They didn't find Geneva, but they did play a part in changing someone's life. Somehow, it was like God was orchestrating everything, every moment.

That night when Elijah laid down, sleep didn't come easily. He kept replaying everything in his mind. From the place she was last seen, to the alley. Something was missing. There was something they missed, he thought. He also knew how Terry was. He always carried things to the very end, never stopping until he got the result he was looking for. This time would not be any different, but doubts were creeping in Elijah's head uninvited, filling the places his positive thoughts were.

Elijah finally found the sleep he truly needed, not going to any other time than the present...just sleep, and waking the following morning, he heard a bunch of commotion going on downstairs.

CHAPTER TWENTY

E lijah hurried and got dressed to go downstairs. He couldn't imagine what was going on, especially at eight o'clock in the morning. They usually let him sleep in, but the echoes of, what sounded like an army at war below him, piqued his curiosity if nothing else but to tell them to shut up.

When he made it to the bottom of the stairs, sheriff Talley, deputy Roberts, and Terry Larey were all there, along with the rest of his crazy crew. Still trying to wake up, Elijah couldn't make out anything, anyone was saying. Everything ran together like a bunch of mumbo jumbo, a mountain of chatter he really didn't feel like running into at such an early hour.

"Goodness gracious everybody," Elijah hollered out, halting them all. "What is going on? Can't a man get some sleep in his own house?"

"We had to come right away Eli," Terry said. "I must've turned my ringer off sometime yesterday by accident."

"Again, I'm gonna ask," Elijah said. "What are you talking about?"

"Look at your phone," the sheriff said.

Stumbling over to the buffet where he laid his phone down the night before, he flipped it open. "I have a voice-mail. You know I don't know how to do all that stuff. That's why I don't have one of them newfangled gadgets all these young folks carry around. Why don't you just tell me?"

The sheriff started, "Sometime after you guys left Shreve-port, Terry and got a voicemail from the lady you met down there, Kimber Moore. She said for you to give her a call. She made it obvious she wanted to talk to you, so I called Terry and we headed straight here," she said. "We're sorry we woke you but figured you wouldn't mind considering it was about Geneva."

Suddenly finding himself fully awake, Elijah listened carefully to everything they were saying. "What's her number?" Elijah said, picking up his phone quickly.

Calling out the phone number, Elijah dialed it and it began to ring. "Hello," a voice answered.

"Is this Kimber?" Elijah asked, a little nervous.

"Yes sir, it is. Am I talking to Elijah?" she asked in a friendly tone.

"You are, and my friends said you wanted to talk to me," Elijah answered, waiting anxiously for her reason for reaching out so soon after they had left.

"Well," she said. "Bennie, Mark, and I thought it was a good idea to circulate the picture you gave us of miss Geneva, thinking we might get some answers that way. I didn't know I'd get someone to call me so quickly."

"Who called and what did they say?" Elijah asked hurriedly.

"A lady I've known for a long time works at several of our hospitals here in Shreveport. She works in the emergency room most of the time and when she saw my post, she immediately called me. She said that some time ago, an older lady was brought in with a head injury," she continued.

"Head injury?" Elijah gasped.

"That's not all," Kimber kept talking. "She had nothing on her, no identification, purse or nothing."

"So, what happened to her?" Elijah asked, hoping the news wasn't something he wanted to hear.

Kimber let out an alarming sigh, "That's where the trail ends. Gloria, my nurse friend, said when the woman did wake up, she couldn't tell anyone her name or where she was from. It's in the time frame you said she went missing and she said she would swear it was your wife going by the picture you gave to Bennie."

"Oh my God," Elijah said, lowering the phone momentarily, trying to take in what she was telling him. "What now? What do we do now?"

"I suppose we try to find out what happened to her after that. Jen was off for a few days after that and when she got back to work, the woman's room was empty. No one would tell her anything because they couldn't. All she found out, was the woman survived," Kimber said.

"What hospital?" he asked, grabbing a pen in the drawer, and writing down the information. "Got it. And thank you Kimber for doing this. You didn't have to."

"By the way Elijah, Bennie wants to talk to you for a minute, if you can," she requested.

"Sure," he said, waiting in line a short time before he heard a man's voice ring in.

"Elijah, I just wanted to say thanks to all of you. If y'all hadn't come here, my life would be different. Mark and Kimber are trying to find me a job. She knows a few people who might need me. She bought me some clothes yesterday, a pair of shoes and a new coat to keep me warm. I can't thank you enough," Bennie said in such a sincere way. "I know you were on a mission for something else, but I thank God, you helped me. I thank God for these kind people who are letting me stay with them. And I pray you find your wife. I just wanted to tell you that sir. You changed my life and told Terry I love my bible. I'll treasure it always."

"I am so happy for you," Elijah smiled, getting a warm feeling inside for being a part of truly helping someone. "People do care about you."

"I know that now," Bennie said. "Please keep us informed on Geneva. We care too."

Elijah hung up the phone and picked up the paper with the hospital's name and address, handing it to the sheriff, "We have to go back," Elijah said. "I think she's alive."

Elijah only thought the place was loud when he first woke up, but right then, everyone began hollering, laughing, and crying, celebrating in every way a person could possibly celebrate.

"Dad," Ella muttered, tears trying to form in her beautiful eyes. "What happened to her?"

"We don't know for sure if it was her, but it could be. And the lady Kimber knows, said the woman came in with a head wound and didn't know anything when she woke up. She did say she was almost positive it was Geneva by looking at her picture," Elijah responded positively, hugging Ella, melting into his daughter with tons of emotion spilling out. "I think it's her honey. I think it's her."

Terry looked at what Elijah had written down, pulled out his phone, and went into the living room. The sheriff followed behind him. It was like Kimber told them the day before, they were on a journey. Ella, Brenda, and Bridget went into the kitchen to make something fast for breakfast. With lots of anxiousness and curiosity filling the air, Elijah knew it wouldn't be long before they were on the road once again.

Elijah went up to his room and sat on his bed for a moment, needing time to think, if only for a few moments. Something told him, he needed time with God.

"Lord, it's me again. I bet you're surprised to hear from me more in a week than you ever heard from me my entire life and I'm sorry for that. God, we got news and you know that, but I'm asking you, please let this woman be Geneva. Please let her be okay. And please, please, help her to remember me. I'd be okay

if she didn't remember the bad things though. I need her back. I need to show her she made a difference in me and in everyone's lives she's touched. I see that now and I need you to walk with me on this journey to find her. Thank you for helping us help others as well. I know you had a hand in it all. I know you have a hand in everything. It's about time I figured that out. I ask this in your precious name...AMEN."

Elijah hurried to get ready, and he could hear everyone scampering around to do the same. He did his best not to get too anxious but every little bit, he could feel his heart start to race. Then the words Monty told him, to breath slow, came to mind. It didn't take long, and Elijah was dressed and putting his shoes on when Caleb knocked at his door.

"Pop," Caleb said. "How you doin'?"

Turning his head to Caleb, "Better than I have been in a long time. I just had a little talk with God, and I think he's got this."

"He always does Pop. He always does," Caleb smiled. "We're ready whenever you are. The girls made up some sausage biscuits to go, so we can get on our way."

Elijah nodded, finished tying his shoes, and went over to the dresser. He picked up the old picture he and Geneva took together years earlier, his hand ran across her face as if she was there, caressing it sweetly. Then spoke aloud softly, "I'm coming, Geneva. I'm coming."

Elijah grabbed his coat hanging on the rack in the corner of the entryway and met everyone out front. Bridget was passing out fresh and hot sausage biscuits to save time, then they were on their way. The sheriff and Terry Road together, as did Jimmy and his bunch. Caleb, Ella, and Elijah loaded up together and joined the three-car convoy back to Shreveport Louisiana. Terry had the name of the hospital that took care of the woman but could do nothing over the phone. She told him, they needed to meet with them in person and have some sort of proof it was the same woman they were looking for.

It was a beautiful morning, but the chill in the air was getting more and more like winter as the days passed. Without even feeling the cold, you could look out and tell it was nippy. From the array of colors in the trees to the leaves all on the ground flying around everywhere, no other evidence was needed.

The drive resembled the day before, Elijah taking in the view to the left and right of him, trying his best not to think of anything else. Like that scripture said, not to worry about tomorrow, Elijah tried his best to obey. Caleb kept his normal chipper attitude with his unique and contagious smile leading him wherever he went. Ella, on the other hand, was in a trans-state, not looking at anything, just staring beyond everything into her thoughts. Elijah knew everything on her mind because the same was trying to wiggle its way into his own.

"Terry needs to slow down," Caleb said. "He's gonna get us all a ticket."

Elijah, laughing, replied quickly, "Well you don't have to speed too. We know the way to the hospital, and he is with a sheriff. All they have to say is we have an emergency."

"For them maybe," Caleb said.

Ella glanced at her husband, shaking her head, and finding a small grin, then
reaching over and patting him on the arm. "You always make me smile."

"I wasn't being funny," he said. "But I'm glad I make you smile."

They started into the long stretch just before getting there and Elijah's mind wandered away with him. It had gotten to be a habit for him, not so much living in the past, but just remembering times he wanted to relive again and again.

Looking at the fields on both sides of the road, watching as the breeze made nature dance around, there was a time that came to the forefront of his thoughts. He and Geneva took a little road trip for the day and decided to go to Shreveport to look around at the boardwalk. She loved the shopping and Elijah loved looking around in the Bass Pro Shop. He never really bought much, but he did like to browse and dream of having lots of the things he saw. Elijah closed his eyes and focused on that day and it came clear as if it were happening all over again.

CHAPTER TWENTY-ONE

"Oh, my goodness honey," Geneva said, walking toward the multitude of stores in front of them. "If I was rich, I'd..."

"Give it all away Geneva," Elijah said, finishing her sentence. "I know you."

"Well," she replied. "You might be right, but I'd sure have a darn good time spendin' some of it. I love all these little shops, but I like them there treasure stores better I think."

"Treasure stores?" Elijah questioned, unsure what she meant.

"You know Elijah, them there stores with antiques and things people threw away just because they're old. There ain't nothing wrong with bein' old. Shoot I'm old and I think I still got a lot a life in me, I can guarantee you that."

Elijah laughed at her but enjoyed the incredibly strong nature she always portrayed since the day he met her; he grabbed her hand.

"What are you a doin'?" Geneva said. "Tryin' to butter me up after laughin' at me. I don't butter that easy buster."

They looked eye to eye, finding something comical in the banter they always found entertaining between them. At times, things she said sounded harsh, but it was never meant that way. People just had to know how to take her. She was never known for subtly in the least and that's what made Elijah fall for her in the first place. The first time he saw her and the first conversation, showed a sass he fell in love with.

"Come on then," she said, wheeling around. "I guess we can go to that durn pro shop you like to meander around. I don't know why you don't ever buy anything."

"I just like to look around," Elijah replied smiling, knowing it would get a rise out of her.

"Looking is for the birds, I like to shop. Let's go shop," she said, dragging him toward the huge store ahead of them.

With the biggest smile on Elijah's face, thinking of such a time, Caleb suddenly slammed on his brakes, throwing him forward a little and jarring Elijah out of his daydreaming state of mind. After being pulled from a happy moment in time, Elijah was faced with reality. There was a chance they might find Geneva, but there was a chance, the woman the nurse was talking about, wasn't her at all. The truth of the matter was, it was no more than a flip of a coin. On the positive side of things, something led them to where they were going, and Elijah had to believe it was something divine. There was a time when he never thought about such, but it was funny how things changed.

"It's just a few blocks away," Caleb said, looking at Ella, then into the rear-view mirror at Elijah. Moments later, he pulled into a parking spot next to Terry. Jimmy pulled up shortly after and everyone got out and congregated outside the hospital doors.

"Who are we looking for?" Elijah asked.

"Her name is Gloria and she's the head nurse on the floor where the woman was being cared for," Terry answered, walking forward and the automatic doors opened. "There's no time like the present."

Terry went straight to the first desk they came to and asked which floor to find Gloria. She was on the third floor and the elevators weren't far from them in the hallway to their right. As the leader he always was, Terry started in that direction. Elijah could feel his nerves starting to get to him, hands beginning to shake, and his heart speeding up a little.

"You alright dad?" Ella asked, noticing the change in him. "You need to sit down?"

"No," Elijah said. "I want to get to that third floor. I'm fine, just anxious."

"One good thing," Terry popped off. "We're in a hospital if you try to have a spell on us again."

Terry eased Elijah's anxiety with humor, and they got in the elevator pushing the number three. For some reason, it seemed like it was going in slow motion, crawling up three flights. A time or two, it made some strange noises like it was creaking on the way up.

"I don't like this," Caleb said, scooting in the corner.

"And you think being in the corner is gonna save you if we plummet back down?" Terry laughed. "You crack me up, son."

The elevator dinged and the doors slowly opened. Caleb shot out of that thing like a scalded cat and everyone couldn't help but laugh. The look on his face was priceless and they all knew Terry would aggravate him every chance he got.

They got out of the elevator and started walking toward a long nurse's station at the end of the hallway, and there sat an older, slender, brown-headed lady.

"Gloria?" Terry asked, seeing her name printed clearly on her badge. "I'm Terry Larey from Texarkana and I understand you helped take care of an older lady, oh, about six weeks ago or so."

"To be honest, that describes lots a folks 'round here sir," she replied.

"This lady had a head injury and didn't know anything when she woke up. She didn't have an identification either," Terry added.

"Well, I'll be," Gloria said. "I'd never forget her."

"What do you mean?" Elijah jumped in, patience not being one of his strong points.

"She might not known who she was, but she sure was a hoot. I swear, I hope I have that kinda attitude when I get her age. That's what keeps you young, you know," she continued.

"If I showed you a picture, could you tell me if it's the woman you saw?" Terry asked, reaching in his pocket.

"I suppose I could. I do remember those eyes of hers. They were the bluest I ever did see, and I told her that every time I went in to check on her," she replied kindly. "She would tell me they came straight from the man upstairs."

Elijah was smiling from the inside out and remembered Geneva saying that same thing many times when people would comment on her eyes. His anxiety was beginning to turn into excitement.

Terry placed the photo in front of the nurse, and she picked it up, smiling from the second she saw it.

"What's her name?" she asked.

"It's Geneva," Elijah answered, waiting. "My wife."

"Now that I think about it, she did kinda look like a Geneva," Gloria said. "This is her. I'm positive." She continued. "I took care of this sweet lady."

"Can you tell us what happened to her?" Ella asked, jumping into the conversation, unable to stay quiet any longer.

"From what I was told, somebody hit her in the head with something and she was found on the sidewalk. I don't remember where at, but I do know, whoever did that to her, meant to do more than hurt her. She was unconscious for several days. To be honest, I didn't think she'd ever wake up, and we couldn't call anybody because we didn't know who she was," Gloria said.

"How long was she here?" Elijah asked.

Thinking, Gloria said, "I guess it was about two weeks. We had to make sure she was okay with no brain bleeds or anything like that. And then the hospital had to find somewhere to place her until they could find someone who knew her."

"Where was she taken?" Terry jumped in.

"Hold on a second," Gloria said, picking up the phone and turning around for a moment. They could hear what she said. "Miss Connie, I have a group of folks here who think they know the woman with head injury a good time back. You remember, the one you transported somewhere else… yes…yes ma'am. Thank you."

The nurse turned back around, and Elijah got an uneasy feeling that maybe the news wasn't so good but did all he could not to keep his thoughts on such negative things. He didn't even want to think about everything she must've gone through, from being the victim of a terrible assault, she didn't deserve, to trying to find out where she belonged. Elijah's guilt began to pile up in every inch of him, punishing himself for not taking her to town the day she asked. And that guilt started to eat away at the good things he had started doing. In a moment of silence, a lifetime of remorse covered him.

"Okay," Gloria said, hanging the phone up. "You all need to go down to the first floor and talk to the hospital administrator. She makes final decisions on everything, and everything goes through her. Her name is Connie Thomason. She's been here for over five years, and she will definitely lead you in the right direction. I'm so sorry I couldn't help more. But I will say this. I hope she is better. She brightened my day every time I went in to see her."

"Hey," Caleb asked when everyone turned to go back to the elevators. "Where are the stairs?"

She pointed Caleb in the direction he needed, and he went.

"Caleb, what are you doing?" Ella asked, watching him go ahead so he could make it down four flights by the time they did by elevator.

"I can't get back on that creaking death trap. I'll meet ya down on the first floor," he said and started down the stairs about the time they got in the elevators.

With a ding, the doors opened, and Elijah stepped out first, looking toward the stairway door to see if Caleb beat them. About that time, before anyone else stepped out of the elevator, Caleb came bursting through the door, hoping he had gotten there first.

"It was close," Caleb said, almost out of breath, gasping as he tried to talk. "Anyway, I needed the exercise."

Ella grabbed Caleb's arm, shaking her head, "Let's go find Mrs. Thomason, and stop acting so crazy. These people might think you need to be locked up or something."

"I am crazy," Caleb replied, smiling. "I'm crazy about you."

"Would you two please concentrate on what we're doing here?" Terry asked, going to where they were told.

Ahead of them, was a long desk with two ladies sitting behind it. They were both elderly, wearing a pink smock a name tag reading volunteer. Terry told them they were needing to see Connie and one of the ladies led them into her office.

"Just have a seat please and she will be in shortly," the lady said. "She is taking care of business down the hall. It shouldn't be long."

Everyone sat and waited as they were asked, and it wasn't but a few minutes when the same lady came back.

"I'm sorry, but it looks like Mrs. Thomason left for lunch. She'll be back in a little over an hour. If you folks want to wait, that's fine. I can also take your number so she can call you when she gets back if you do leave," the lady said

Elijah got up and gave her his number as well as Terry's just in case they went somewhere for a bit. She took it and put it on her desk, and sat down, continuing to work.

"Lunch sounds good," Caleb said, not shocking anyone.

"I'm with Caleb," Jimmy agreed, looking around to see if everyone wanted to do the same.

"I guess we could," Elijah said. "It sure beats sitting here for an hour or more waiting. Where yall want to go?"

They discussed a few places to eat, from Mexican to Italian and everything in between, and they finally agreed on a place. It was a restaurant famous for their margaritas, although none of them were much on drinking, Superior Bar & Grill. It wasn't too far off, on Line Avenue. That tiny bit of breakfast the girls whipped up quickly if you want to call it that, didn't go far, and they all needed nourishment to make it through the rest of the day. Unsure of what would unfold once they met Connie, they needed something to occupy themselves until the next step in the mystery they were trying to uncover. As close as they were to finding the truth, it was possible it wasn't her at all.

Since they didn't need to take all three vehicles, they left parked, and they piled into two. Terry led the way to the restaurant and going on eleven o'clock, most places probably weren't too busy just yet and they wanted to get back within the hour. Terry pulled into the parking lot and Caleb followed behind. Getting out, never being there before, Elijah looked around, only two or three other vehicles there at the time, noticing the character of the place.

The walkway was made from random-sized natural stone pieces, fit together like a puzzle perfectly. There was a bench in front of each large window in the front with two large pots with a small tree growing from each one. The Dark green awning reaching out in front gave it an inviting feel.

"After you," Terry said, opening the door and letting the girls go in first, then the rest and following in the rear.

"Welcome to Superior Bar & Grill," A nice, neatly dressed young man said. "How many?

"Nine please," Terry replied.

"Right this way," he said, grabbing enough menus for everyone.

After getting settled at their table, Elijah couldn't help but look around. There were string lights on the ceiling all around them, blinking different colors, and the décor was interesting. People started sifting in after they arrived, but their waiting was prompt and very friendly. Everyone placed their orders, and it didn't take long before their food came out sizzling hot.

"I was starving," Caleb said, grabbing his utensils.

"Wait," Elijah said. "We need to say grace."

"May I?" Terry asked kindly, everyone nodding yes. *"Lord, thank you for this group of folks I'm lucky enough to be sharing this journey with. Please God, give us direction and the peace we need that can only come from you. Bless this food for the nourishment of our bodies and thank you for always being there when we need you, Lord. I ask this in your son's name... AMEN."*

"Amen," said in unison, then they dove into their plates.

"You not getting a drink?" Elijah asked Terry.

Terry laughed, "I'm driving the sheriff around. Now, how would that look?"

Elijah grinned at his answer and brought up a memory that came to the forefront of his thoughts. "You know, Geneva was never a drinker, but she did love a good Long Island Iced Tea for some reason."

"Mama?" Ella asked like she didn't have a clue.

"Yep, your mama," Elijah started laughing. "And I swear, I never understood it. She never drank, but every once in a blue moon, we'd go somewhere, and she'd get her a Long Island Iced Tea and wouldn't even get tipsy."

"Lord help us all if she did get drunk," Jimmy joined in. "As crazy as she already is, can you imagine how alcohol would make her act."

"I bet all those stories she told us all those years would grow into many more, some she might've left out in the first place," Ella said. "But right now, I'd like to hear a few."

It didn't take long until they finished their meal, and the waiter came with the ticket. Terry snatched it when Elijah tried to reach for it.

"Nope, Eli. It's on me," he said digging his wallet from his pocket.

"I'm not destitute now Terry. I can pay for my own," Elijah replied, still trying to get the ticket from him.

"Just say thank you, my friend," Terry smiled. "Just say thank you."

"I guess I wouldn't want to steal a blessing from you now, would I?" Elijah aggravated.

"No, you wouldn't," Terry said, paying and leaving the tip.

Elijah's phone started to ring, and he answered.

"Is this Mr. James," a woman's voice said on the other end of the line.

"Yes, ma'am it is," he answered. "Who is this?"

"I'm Connie Thomason and your number. You came by trying to find your wife?" she continued.

"Yes ma'am, I did. Do you have any information?" He asked, feeling his anxiety starting to get his heart racing, trying hard to stay calm.

"Please come to my office," Connie said. "I'll find her file, assuming it is your wife. I can't tell you much over the phone. I need to see the picture you brought as well."

"We'll be there shortly," Elijah said, hanging up the phone.

CHAPTER TWENTY-TWO

E lijah told them what she said, and it didn't take long to get in the cars and make their way back to the hospital. The entire way, Elijah's mind started going in every direction. He kept thinking, maybe it wasn't her and he was getting his hopes up for nothing. He thought what if it was her and she didn't know him. Every idea circling in his head started to fill the positive thinking from earlier. He knew what she would tell him. She would say *"It's that ole devil a talkin' to ya Elijah and don't you listen to the devil."*

"Dang these lights," Caleb said, aggravated at getting stopped at every intersection. "Don't these people know we're in a hurry?"

"We'll get there," Ella said. "We wouldn't be here if we weren't supposed to be…right dad?"

"Right," Elijah said, staring out the window at all the tall buildings in the distance and places all around them. "We're supposed to be here."

"What's wrong dad?" Ella turned around and asked.

"What if it's not even her Ella? What if we are going on a wild goose chase and we come up empty and I go back home alone? I don't think I could handle that," Elijah answered, looking more upset with each word spoken.

"You can't think that way dad," Ella said, doing her best to comfort him. "Besides, you heard what that nurse, Gloria said. She said it was mom…"

"How can she remember that far back Ella? Shoot, I can barely remember what I did yesterday. How can she know when it's been almost two months since she saw her?" Elijah replied in a gloomy manner. "I'm just scared."

"I know you are. We all are dad, but…"

"But nothing," Elijah said raising his tone a bit. "This is a woman who I didn't really appreciate when I had her and if I do get her back, will I still be that same person?"

"You're not the same person," Ella smiled. "We all see the difference in you. Ever since that day at church, you've been kinder, sweeter, and very considerate. No offence dad, but you were never really like that before. God changed you and you have to believe that."

About then, Caleb pulled into the parking spot not far from the front door of the hospital. Terry had already arrived and was sitting in his truck waiting. Elijah had a shakiness running through his entire body, from his head to his toes, the kind making it hard to breathe. Then he remembered what that kind paramedic, Monty told him, to breath slow. That's exactly what he did. For a few moments, he sat there, even though everyone was waiting on him. Somehow, he knew he had to find peace inside. With that in mind, he closed his eyes, kept breathing slow an, said a silent prayer, only he and God could hear.

"God, it's me again. I know you already know why I'm calling on you again, and I'm sorry it seems I'm always asking for something, but Lord, I need you now. I need you to help me find peace, whether we find Geneva or not. I know whatever happens is in your plan and I have to accept it. Please, Lord, give me the strength to follow through this crazy journey you've sent me on. I know it has happened for a reason and you orchestrated it all. Thank you for everything you do, and I ask this is Jesus' name… AMEN."

Elijah opened his eyes and strangely enough, almost instantly, his shakiness was gone, and he held a peacefulness inside of him, he didn't think he would feel at that moment, in that place. Then he looked up and nodded to God as if to say *thank you*. He looked out the car window, and everyone was together by Terry's truck. For some reason, they all knew he needed a moment, and no one interrupted him when he had to have that little talk with the man upstairs.

Elijah got out, straightened his back, and stood tall as he could, once more whispering a thank you to God, and walking toward Ella.

"I'm ready," Elijah said. "Let's go find your mama."

Ella took him by the hand, and said, "Let's go find her."

They trailed behind everyone, walking hand in hand through the front doors, turning toward Mrs. Thomason's office. Although Elijah was still scared of the outcome, something told him everything would be okay. The old Elijah would've been complaining and causing all kinds of trouble, but the new Elijah found a new approach to life.

Terry walked up to the lady at the desk and said something to her. She picked up then phone, then hung it up right after. "Mrs. Thomason will see you now. But only two of you can go in. There isn't enough room for everyone if the rest of you don't mind waiting out here?"

"You and Elijah go in," Terry told Ella. "We'll be out here if you need us."

"Thank you for all you've done Terry," Ella said, giving him a sincere embrace, showing her gratitude.

"I do what I'm supposed to do Ella," he replied. "And I hope I've helped."

The door to the office opened and there stood a pretty lady with blonde hair and eyes that would light up a room. Her smile was comforting even before she said a single word.

"Mr. James?" she said.

"Yes," Elijah answered. "And my daughter Ella."

"Come on in," she said, then nodding and smiling at the others before closing the door behind her.

All three of them went into her office and sat down, Elijah noticed how personally the room was decorated. It was filled with family pictures and a calming tranquil scent floated all around them. She had all sorts of certificates hanging on the walls and the lighting was dim, but it gave a feeling of home at the same time.

"Is that your family?" Elijah asked as she pulled out a few files, placing them on her desk.

"It sure is," she replied in a soothing tone. "That's my husband Kitt and my daughter Kaitlyn, and I must stay they are somethin' else. Keeps me on my toes to say the least."

"It looks like your husband and daughter are close," Elijah said, continuing to make small talk to calm his own nerves.

"I'll tell you this much," Connie said. "When Kaitlyn went off to college, I thought Kitt was going to climb in her luggage and go with her."

Ella and Elijah found themselves laughing at such a funny story, and Ella chimed in, "Well, I love my dad too, so I understand. That's very sweet."

Connie took in a deep breath and let it out, then started, "So, sometime back, we got a patient in with a head injury. There was no identification, of course, as you know, and we took very good care of her. Gloria, upstairs, was especially fond of her. She told me you showed her a picture of your wife."

"Yes ma'am," Elijah said, his hands shaking as he answered.

"Call me Connie please," she said with a chuckle. "Ma'am sounds like I'm old and I like to think I'm still a young lady, even though time is moving on."

"Connie," he replied with a smile. "Here it is."

Elijah lifted the picture from his wallet and placed it in her hands. She flipped open the other file to her left and began to smile. Elijah couldn't take her expression in any other way, than positive.

"Oh, my goodness," Connie said, showing excitement. "God is good Mr. James."

Scooting up where he was sitting at the edge of his seat, "Is it my Geneva? Please tell me it's her."

"Yes," Ella said, putting her arm around her dad. "Is it my mama?"

Almost in tears, Connie turned the file around. In it, was a picture clipped to the top of it. It was the one they took at the hospital before she left. It was those same ice blue eyes Elijah fell in love with the first time he saw her, and the same smile she kindly wore around everywhere like a beautiful outfit.

"Yes Mr. James," Connie started.

"Call me Elijah, please," he said, his emotions taking over.

"Yes, Elijah, it's Geneva," she said, reaching for tissues at the edge of her desk, giving one to each of them and keeping one for herself. "I prayed for a long time to find her family. I never did lose hope."

Elijah, resting his face in his hands, a flood of tears came raining down, so much he couldn't speak. Each time he tried, it was interrupted with the feeling of gratefulness and made him live in the moment a little while longer. All he could say was, "My God...my God."

"That's who brought you here, Elijah. It couldn't have been anyone else," Connie said, getting up and going around to him. "Can I give you a hug?"

With no words, only a nod, she kneeled and hugged him like she'd known him forever. She cried with him, and his tears rested on her shoulder. When she got up and went back to her seat, wiping her own tears at the same time, she opened the other file once more.

"Would you like to know where Geneva is Elijah?" Connie asked, laughing a little from the happiness lingering in the room, knowing his answer before she ever asked.

"I would love to know Connie," Elijah replied, laughing with her, joy taking over any pessimistic thoughts previously lingering.

She got herself together, and took a piece of paper, writing down the name of a home she was transported to, with the address and phone number.

"She's at the Brook Hollow Nursing Home," Connie said. "I'll give them a call and let them know you're coming."

Elijah looked up for a moment, and asked, "Is she okay?"

"Well," Connie said with a smile. "I don't usually make it my normal policy to check on everyone we release from here, but with this lovely lady, I did. For a while she didn't remember much, but her spirit was incredible. If she ever told them her name, I never knew about it, but health wise, she's healed perfectly. And I hope they found whoever attacked her. A part of me wanted to go and search for him myself."

"Thank you so much," Elijah said, standing up and extending his hand. "You're an angel."

"You have no idea how much of a pleasure this has been for me to meet you and especially find this incredible lady," Connie replied. "I wish you all good luck."

"She's my good luck charm miss Connie," Elijah said, wiping the tears remaining on his face and opening her office door, then turning back to her. "You have answered a prayer."

"No, God answered a prayer through me," Connie said, her radiant smile showing.

Elijah and Ella went out to where everyone was waiting, and Elijah's tears were still showing. Terry got up slowly and walked over to him, placing his hand on Elijah's shoulders.

"I'm sorry Elijah," Terry said, assuming those were tears of sadness falling.

"I'm not," Elijah said, letting his smile shine. "I'm going to get my wife."

Everyone in the hospital probably thought a party was going on with all the whooping and hollering, laughing, and crying going on amidst them. Caleb pulled Ella in, both letting all the emotions from that moment, sink in, thanking God every second. Jimmy, Brenda, Tom, and Bridget joined in on the love, and they realized, the journey wasn't for naught.

"She's at the Brook Hollow Nursing Home," Elijah said. "Mrs. Connie is calling them now to let them know we're on our way."

"I can't wait to see her," Jimmy announced energetically.

Elijah pausing for a moment, and took a few steps away from everyone, then turned back around. "Would you mind if me and Ella do this alone?" he requested as nicely as he could, trying not to hurt anyone's feelings. "I just feel like…"

Caleb stopped him before he could say another word, "I think you and Ella should be the ones to go. I'll ride back with the others."

Terry and the rest nodded in agreement and got closer, all hugging Elijah so he'd know they were there if he needed them.

"Come on Caleb," Jimmy said. "Let them two go bring Geneva back."

Caleb hugged Ella one more time and handed her the car keys, then followed behind the others, turning back once, blowing a kiss to her on his way out.

"It's like a dream dad," Ella said, standing still. "I feel like I'm going to wake up in a minute and it was all a dream."

"You're not dreaming honey," Elijah said. "And I don't have to dream anymore either. I'll have the object of my dream with me again, and the next time she wants to go somewhere, I'm takin' her."

"What are we waiting for?" Ella said, lifting the keys up. "Let's go."

As they were on the way in, hand in hand, they left that place in better spirits than when they arrived. When they got there, doubts were holding their minds hostage but leaving, only hope prevailed. They got in the car and Elijah turned on the radio, finally wanting to listen to music, rather than sit in silence.

Ella put the address in her phone for directions to where her mama was, and it wasn't far away, only ten minutes or so. The ride was the most peaceful one in several months, as joy was the only feeling in and around them. At one point, Elijah and Ella caught themselves singing along with the song playing.

"We're really going to see her dad," Ella said, unable to wipe the smile from her face.

"Just like Kimber told me at the bookstore," Elijah said. "It's been a journey, but one I'm glad I took."

Ella pulled up to the nursing home, and there were beautiful trees all around it as well as sitting areas everywhere. Ella parked in the first spot by the door. When she turned off the engine, all they could do was look at one another for a moment. Elijah got out and met Ella as she made her way around.

Slowly but eagerly, they went inside. Elijah's nerves were shaky, but not in a bad way. For once, his anxiousness was because he was looking forward to something, rather than dreading something. When they reached the first nurses' station, he found someone to ask for directions.

"Ma'am," he said, waving down the first nurse he saw. "I think Connie Thomason called you from…"

"We've been praying to find her family," the nurse said, waving over the head nurse turning the corner. "I'm sorry sir, what was your name again."

"Elijah James," he answered. "I'm her husband."

The head nurse made her way to them and shoot Elijah's hand, "It is such a pleasure to meet you sir."

CHAPTER TWENTY-THREE

"**M**iss Jane is right this way," the nurse said, walking down the hallway.

"Miss Jane?" Ella asked, eyebrows lowered.

"We never knew her name, so that's what we called her, especially since that's what it sounded like she said her name was. Sometimes she'd talk to us about things we figured was her life, but nothing ever came together enough to fill the whole puzzle. So, we just listened. She's a spry one, I must say. All the nurses fight to sit with her because she's so entertaining to talk to."

"What did she talk about?" Elijah added.

"God," she said. "Always talking about God, Jesus, and her cross."

"The cross," Ella smiled, picturing the one they bought on the way to Hot Springs.

"Every day she's been getting better. We all knew one day she'd snap out of it. After that knock her head, it's a wonder she's still with us. I have to say she's a tough one."

The nurse stopped in front of room One twenty-three, "Here we are," the nurse said, motioning they could go in.

"What if it's not her dad?" Ella said, beginning to weep on his shoulder.

Finally, they slowly pushed the door open, the smell nursing homes always had, floated all around them. That's why Elijah told Ella never to put him in one of those places. He said he didn't want to die in a place like that.

They eased around the corner, and Ella fell to her knees, crying and Elijah stood there like he was in a trans, afraid of the emotions running through his heart and mind. It was his Geneva, lying there looking helpless when the only thing he remembered about her was a woman full of energy and attitude. Her eyes were closed, and her hands rested beside her. With such a peaceful look across her beautiful face, Elijah began to cry.

Ella got up and put her arms around Elijah and began to smile bigger than she had since the day her mama went missing several months earlier. "We found her...we found her dad. It's really mama."

No words came from Elijah's mouth, only happy tears found their way down his cheeks filled with lines from living. Then he looked up. He stared up at the ceiling like someone was there, knowing God was for sure. The silence seemed welcomed to Elijah at that moment, something necessary and sacred.

"What is it?" Ella asked sweetly, rubbing his arm in comfort.

"It's God," Elijah whispered. "It's nothing but God."

"You're right. He's been taking care of her all this time until we could find her. She's been waiting for us."

"You know Ella, she's told me for years how he's always with me and that he takes care of us, but I never believed her. I was too doggone stubborn to listen and too selfish to care," he said, his eyes never glancing away from the woman he loved in front of him.

"You believe now, dad That's what's important," Ella said, hugging him once more.

Both Ell and Elijah noticed her begin to wiggle around slightly, Geneva's eyes began to open, slowly, coming out of peaceful sleep. They could tell her eyes were trying to focus for a moment, and when they did, she began to cry. Geneva didn't say a word, she just cried. Ella and Elijah each took a side of the bed and rushed to her.

"Mama," Ella said, resting her head on Geneva's chest, embracing her. "We didn't know. We couldn't find you."

In a sleepy voice, "They kept askin' me for my name and I kept tellin' them James, but nothing else came to mind. I barely remember bein' hit over the head from some hoodlum and ending up here. They've been callin' me Jane ever since," she said, then she turning to Elijah.

He pulled up a chair and rested his head on the bedrail, "Please forgive me," he begged. "You deserve so much better than me Geneva…so much better"

Geneva started crying with him, reaching, and resting her hand on his, "Elijah, look at me."

His eyes practically swollen from the tears and emotion rushing out of him, he did as she asked, "I'm lucky, you've been mine from the first time we met. Nobody's perfect, but we can work on bein' that way. Whatcha think?"

"I'll work on it. I promise," he said, standing up, leaning over, and kissing her like he dreamed of since she left. All those dreams seemed to come to life before his eyes, but this time, he wouldn't wake up from it. For the first time in a while, she was right in front of him, flesh, and bones.

Elijah could feel eyes watching, and they all looked toward the doorway. In the hallway, was more than half a dozen facility workers, nurses, and a doctor. They all wore smiles of excitement and joy, and a few were even clapping, happy she finally found who she belonged to.

The doctor walked on in and reached out his hand, "I'm Dr. Mitchell. I've been taking care of this sweet young lady here. She's definitely a handful."

"You betcha," Geneva chimed in.

"We don't know how she ended up this far from home or ended up here, but I have to say, she has blessed all our lives. There's not a single person here, she hasn't made a difference in. And now, we know her first name."

"It's Geneva," she spoke out with vigor, enthusiasm oozing without a doubt.

The doctor grinned, but emotional at the same time, he continued, "We thought she was saying her name was Jane, but she was telling us her last name, James. I'm so very sorry. We should've paid more attention. We might have found you sooner."

"Well," Elijah said, still holding Geneva's hand, "We have her back now."

"It'll take a few days to get her paperwork done to release her and you'll have to keep a good eye on her. She's come a long way and I think she's well on the road to recovery, but she did take a nasty lick on the head, and it takes time to heal," the doctor said.

"She'll be taken care of," Elijah replied, looking at the doctor once more.

"Miss Geneva," Dr. Mitchell said, going over and gently shaking her hand. "Thank you."

"For what honey?"

"For being you. You've been you even when you didn't know who that was. And we all love who you are," he said kindly. "You kept things lively around here. I hate to see you go, but glad you found your family. I'll get your paperwork started."

"Thank you, doctor," Geneva said, flashing her exceptional smile, then turning her attentions to Elijah. "When we head home, y'all think I could drive?" she said, laughing at herself afterward.

The feeling floating all around, was a combination of happiness, gratitude, love, hope and relief, all balled up together. The bitterness Elijah held onto for so long, dissipated the very moment he saw her, the anger he always held on to tightly, immediately got covered with love instead.

It reminded him of a scripture she always quoted him, *Love covers a multitude of sins,* and he believed it. Love was all he could grasp onto or feel, sitting next to her once again. Anger had no place and bitterness was surely not allowed in such an instance.

"Where's...where's..." Geneva started saying, looking into Ella's eyes, showing how her mind wasn't completely back just yet.

"Caleb?" Ella said, finishing her sentence.

"Yes honey, I'll get it I promise," she laughed. "This here ole' brain a mine might need a little time gettin' it back together."

"He's home waiting for us," Ella smiled. "Along with Brenda, Jimmy, Bridget, Tom, Terry Larey and sheriff Nancy Talley."

"My lands," she gasped, surprised at the people she mentioned. "What in the world? I haven't seen Elijah's sisters in quite some time. And why is..."

"We've all been looking for you mama," Ella responded happily. "Terry and the sheriff played a big part finding you. Your car was found in Baton Rouge, and it all went from there. It's been a wild ride. Caleb is excited to see you mama," Ella continued. "Dad thought it best that we be the ones to come here."

Geneva laughed, "I'll tell ya one thing. If that crew had a come down these halls, I imagine they'd a called the law. They don't go nowhere quietly, especially that Jimmy."

Elijah and Ella listened to Geneva carry on like nothing ever happened, and they just sat and listened to her. Hearing her voice was like music to his ears, and he couldn't get enough.

"Caleb still gonna write that book he talked about all the time?" Geneva asked, surprised so much was coming to her at one time. "He's got an imagination from what I remember."

"More than you think," Elijah laughed. "Boy, have we got some stories to tell you."

"Well, I betcha you do, but let me get my wits about me first. Then we'll get all caught up. I'm just ready to git outa here."

About then, the doctor came back in. He said he needed one of them to sign some papers and they would be able to get her released the following morning. The smile wiped across Geneva's face was irremovable. Her joy enclosed her entire being and that gleam in her smile lit up the room like the brightest light of the sun.

"By golly, I can't wait," Geneva said, her energy beginning to show without a doubt.

Dr. Mitchell stopped at the doorway, and turned back, "Don't be running no marathon's now Miss Geneva."

"Not on the first day doc," she replied, her old familiar humor ringing out.

He left the room and left Ella and Elijah alone with the one person they had missed for several months. The dimly lit room with little décor and one small television on the wall, was all she had.

"I wish I had…" Elijah started.

"Ain't gonna accept no wishin'," Geneva said, with attitude. "This is a good moment…enjoy it, Elijah. That's been your problem for a long time now. You don't enjoy things. We ain't no spring chickens, but we still got some livin' to do."

"Yes ma'am," he said humoring her.

"That's more like it," she said, then looking over to Ella. "Now that's how you make a man mind girl…take notes."

They were there for a while, but noticing how late it was, Ella turned to her dad, "You want to head home and we'll come back in the morning...you know to bring her some clothes to change into."

"I'm not going anywhere," he replied, clutching Geneva's hand as if she would disappear if he let go.

"But dad," she started.

"The company would be nice Ella," Geneva spoke up. "B'sides, I bet you and Caleb wouldn't mind a little alone time...you know what I mean? That is, if you can escape the rest bedding down there."

"Mama," Ella said, shocked she'd say such a thing, but not really shocked at the same time. She always was a spitfire and very outspoken, so she should've expected such.

With no more arguments, she kissed her mama and hugged her dad, "See you two in the morning," she said, winking as to say *behave*.

Geneva winked right back at her, answering her unspoken remark. When Ella was gone, the quiet of the room took over for a bit, like God was doing his magic. Truth be known, he did his magic, leading them back to her. Nothing else could explain it.

"We were sitting outside the other day and Ella brought up the crosses on the swing," he said. "I couldn't talk about it then. I was too angry you were gone."

"Not gone," she said. "Just here...and yes I remember the day you made that thing for me. You didn't want to, especially the cross I wanted you to carve into each armrest. You gave me all kind a fits about that. You remember?"

"Yes, I remember," he said grinning but feeling ashamed. "You told me to follow the cross and you'll always find your way home."

"Yeppers, I did," she responded in her own little language. "And it will too."

"I'm starting to believe you Geneva. After all these years, I'm starting to believe."

"I don't know why you wouldn't Elijah," she said. "Gods saved you more times than you'll ever know. I swear, with your ornery nature, arguin' and fightin' attitude, it's a wonder you didn't get a hold of the wrong person and them beat you to death."

"I wasn't that bad now Geneva," he said, almost taking it back in the same breath.

She didn't respond. All she had to do was give him a particular look, the one he knew to avoid or shut up talking, one of the two. She laid her head back on the pillow and took in a deep breath and let it out slowly.

"I swear I keep thinkin' I'm a dreamin'," she said, staring up at the ceiling. "I've dreamed a this day since my mind started gettin' right again. I never thought a knock on the head would make you forget so much."

Elijah pulled the recliner chair over close to her bed, holding her hand tightly, "You're not dreaming. I'm here."

Obvious they were both very tired, the moon shone through the window to their right, putting off a hypnotizing glow in the room, lulling them to sleep. He rested his head where his eyes could be on her should he wake up, while holding her hand…making sure he really wasn't dreaming, and they both found peace for the night.

Although those types of chairs were never the most comfortable to sleep in, Elijah found the best rest he had in months. A few times through the night, his eyes would pop open and look to make sure she was still there, then close again, never letting go of her hand. Finally, morning approached, and he was awakened by a loud noise, hearing nurses holler out that someone was coding.

CHAPTER TWENTY-FOUR

"Geneva," Elijah yelled, jumping up from his chair, only to be relieved by her lying there staring at him. "Oh, thank God."

"Now that's somethin' I've waited to hear you say for a long time," she said, grinning from ear to ear.

"Woman, you are something else," Elijah replied, giving a sign of relief.

"That's what I've been told all my life," she said. "So, I guess it must be true. Now, where's that daughter of ours? I'm ready to fly this joint and get back home."

"I imagine her, and Caleb will be here soon. She's probably making sure the house is nice and tidy for you. She knows how picky you are," he smiled.

"I betcha Caleb and Jimmy done ate anything left in that there kitchen. Whatcha think?" she said chuckling as she spoke.

Elijah, about to make a witty remark, Dr. Mitchell walked in. He stood there, tall with wide shoulders, dark hair, tanned skin, and the oddest color green eyes anyone had ever seen, and he went to Geneva's bedside. "Well, I guess you're leaving us Mrs. James."

"It was Geneva yesterday, now it's Mrs. James. I see how you're gonna be. What's your first name?" she responded in a snappy tone, but playful at the same time.

"Dylan," he said.

"Oh, you have one of them there movie star names," she said, letting her laughter fill the room. "You know, one a those players who gets any ole gal he wants."

"I can tell you were a rounder in your day," he said, grinning at her comment, not sure he'd just opened a can of worms. "And I'm not a player, I'm a doctor."

"In my day," she said, acting offended. "I tell you one thing mister; I can keep up with the best of 'em. I mow the yard, bushhog our property, garden, and anything else you can think of. Whatever a man can do, I can do just as good as better. You can bet on that."

The doctor looked toward Elijah to see his response, and he nodded a definite *YES!* Dr. Mitchell couldn't help but be amused by her spirited ways. Her colorful personality radiated all around and gave that place a little liveliness for the time being, at least until she was gone.

"You know what Geneva?" he said, crossing his arms. "It's my guess, if that guy hadn't hit you over the head, you would be out bush hogging a field right now."

"If it needed it, yes I would," she said, sitting straight up in the bed like she was ready to jump down and take off running toward home.

"Well, you take care of yourself," he said, handing the papers to Elijah. "You are all set…and again, thank you for being you."

It wasn't often Geneva was speechless, but he caused it then. She didn't know what she had done to be such an inspiration, but no matter, she was grateful to be going home.

"That blame girl better hurry it up," Geneva said, showing her anxiousness to get back home.

Elijah picked up a bible from the table next to her bed, handing it to her, "Read to me," he quietly requested.

With a look like she thought he might be playing a joke on her, "You want me to read the bible to you?"

"I do," he said, sitting back calmly.

Excitement for his request, her fingers began to thumb through the pages hurriedly, hoping he wouldn't change his mind, unaware of his change of attitude and beliefs. Then she landed on a set of Scriptures that meant a lot to her. She had read them to him before, but he didn't listen, not in the right way.

"Let's see here now," she said, flipping the pages another time or two until she stopped. "In Philippian's 4:6 it says, *"Do not be anxious about anything, but in everything by prayer and supplication with thanksgiving let your requests be made known to God."*

"What does that mean?" Elijah asked sincerely.

Geneva rested the sacred book in her lap, "Honey, it means stop worryin' about everything and give it all to the Almighty God. You see, if you keep your worries, he can't take care of them. You gotta give it all to him and trust he's gonna take care of it."

"Is that how you got through this?"

"You betcha it is," she said, giving a quick nod. "If I didn't have God lookin' out for me, you woulda never found me. He led you here honey. It sure wasn't by accident."

"Knock, knock," a voice said, Caleb and Ella, walking in, all smiles.

Caleb ran over and hugged Geneva and kissed her on the cheek. His infectious positive attitude, jumped on everyone as he went on and on about this and that, trying to make up for the lost time in a matter of minutes.

"Okay, okay honey," Geneva said, we can talk on the way home. "Grab my things."

Caleb followed orders like a pro, knowing she and Ella were pretty much the same when they wanted something. "Yes ma'am."

After gathering her things, they started down the hallway, and everyone in the place started clapping. A few even came over and hugged Geneva before she could make her way outside. Dr. Mitchell stood at the end of the nurse's station and saluted Geneva like she was a sergeant or something. Finally, they were headed home. It's like it was the beginning of a new life for everyone.

Ella couldn't help but turn around over and over, making sure her mama was still there. In all the time Ella did her best to keep Elijah positive, her thoughts weren't, so seeing her mama's face made everything, worth it.

Elijah brought up what happened to Geneva but did it carefully. From what the police said, she stopped somewhere because she was lost, and that's when a guy came from behind and hit her. He took the car, and it was never found from the information they were given. At the end of the day, there was no way for anyone to know who she was until someone found her.

"So," Caleb said seriously. "What's for lunch?"

Ella did her usual, hitting the arm when he'd say something stupid, but then again, he probably was already hungry. Geneva started laughing and couldn't stop. Whether she was thinking about all she missed or just that moment in time, it was obvious, she found her happy place once again.

Just over an hour drive and they were finally pulling down the long dirt driveway off the main road, leading to their house. Geneva got emotional looking in the direction of home. There it stood, grand. Her eyes were fixed on the place, probably reliving memories she never wanted to forget.

"You okay mama?" Ella asked.

"Fine honey. Just never thought I'd ever see it again. I really didn't," Geneva responded in a reminiscent way.

"We never gave up Geneva," Elijah said. "Well, maybe a few times I…"

"I understand honey," she said. "How could any of you know? The important thing is that we're home now."

They climbed out of the car and Caleb grabbed up Geneva's things. Elijah helped her out, although anyone could see she didn't appear to need it. It didn't matter though. Elijah wanted to show how much he loved and missed her.

The sheriff's car was parked on the right side of the house and another car sat right next to it. Geneva knew she was going to have a welcoming committee waiting for her as soon as she walked in the door.

With a pep in her step, like she was never bedridden, Geneva hopped out and scurried up the steps to the porch, plopping down on the swing in the corner. Her fingers automatically outlined the cross on the armrest as she always did when she sat there.

"My swing," she said. "Oh, good Lord I missed my swing."

Elijah came up the steps and went over, sitting next to her, "It missed you too Geneva," Elijah said. Without missing a beat, his arm swing over her, his hand resting on her shoulder, and pulling her close to him.

"Don't you be gettin' frisky now? The young'uns are here," she said, giving him an elbow nudge sporting the smile they all loved.

"Mama," Ella said. "I swear you are one of a kind."

"You better betcha this world would be in trouble if God had made two a me," she answered.

"Come on Caleb," Ella said, grabbing Caleb's hand. "Let's see what everyone wants, and we'll start lunch."

She didn't have to tell him twice. That crazy grin of his immediately came out and he followed behind her without hesitation.

"Them two are somethin' else," Geneva said, looking around the property, taking it all in. "I sure missed this place, Elijah. I thought I'd never see it again. And would ya look at them there hills. Beautiful…"

"You're here now, and that's all that matters," Elijah whispered.

They watched the trees dance around with the orchestra of the wind inspiring it all and sat there taking in the moment. Elijah started thinking back to different bible verses Geneva had tried her best to drum into his head for years. But suddenly, they all came rushing in.

"What was the bible verse talking about how short a time we have?" he asked, as sincere as he had done earlier about her reading to him.

With the most peaceful tone, Geneva answered, *"Why, you do not even know what will happen tomorrow. What is your life? You are a mist that appears for a little while and then vanishes...James 4:14"*

He turned her to him and gently kissed her forehead, then her lips. "This is my life and I thank God for it, for this moment and for you. If it were my last, I'd die a happy man," Elijah said.

Time seemed to fly by and before they knew it, Ella poked her head out and said for them to come and eat. Elijah took Geneva by the hand, "Shall we?" Elijah said in a gentleman-like fashion.

"We shall," she answered, lacing her fingers with his, not sure what to make of Elijah's newfound way of thinking.

They walked inside, and once more Geneva's eyes lit up, so happy to be back in the place she always called home, from the first time she ever laid eyes on it. She looked around to make sure everything was, as it had always been, she was more than pleased to be there. Then, turning to glance in the living room, a line of folks came to her, passing out hugs and kisses galore.

"Geneva," Terry said, "I sure am glad you made it home. I don't know how Eli would've made it without you."

"Mean as that ole codger is, he'd a been just fine," she laughed, then turning to hug Brenda and Bridget. It was better than a family reunion, it was a homecoming in a place filled with love.

"What about me Geneva?" Jimmy said, shoving his way through everyone.

"Jimmy, I always got a hug for you," she said, looking into his baby blue eyes. "Thank you all for staying with Elijah. Ya'll didn't have to."

"Yes, we did," Jimmy said. "Yes, we did."

"I smell somethin' good a cookin'," Geneva said, wheeling around, heading straight to the kitchen. Caleb already found his place at the table with a glass of sweet tea and Ella was by the stove fixing everyone's plates.

"Let me help you, honey," Geneva said, going toward Ella.

"No mama," Ella stopped her. "Let me do this for you. We can't stay much longer, and I want to serve you."

"I'm a not complainin' honey," she said. "Bring on the vittles."

"That's what I'm talkin' about Ma," Caleb added, sitting there with a fork in one hand and knife in the other.

His silly antics tickled all their funny bones and they all belted out laughing over him. For the first time in a while, they all laughed together.

Ella sat down after serving everyone their plates, "Let's say grace," Ella said, reaching for them to hold hands.

Elijah surprised Geneva and spoke up. "Do you mind if I do the honors?"

Ella and Geneva looked at one another, smiled, nodded a definite yes, and they all bowed their heads.

Elijah took in a deep breath, unsure of what he was going to say, but he found the words. *"Dear God, Elijah here. I know I always said you didn't know me, but I guess you did. You knew I needed my Geneva back and you came through. God, I'm sorry for doubting you. I thank you for this time with my family. If it wasn't for you, it wouldn't be happening. Lord, please stay with us, guide us all, and keep us together. Please bless this food and I'll never doubt you again....Amen."*

A peaceful silence came over the room for just a moment after, like God was joining them for supper. Elijah's attitude had truly been transformed into something new and inspired. His eyes beamed with happiness and love, just like the day at the church, the anger he always carried around, was gone. The selfish demeanor he always portrayed, nonexistent. Overall, the old Elijah went away, replacing him, was the Elijah God always intended him to be.

"I always knew," Geneva whispered to Elijah.

"Knew what dear?" he responded sweetly.

"I knew you'd believe one day. I just had to be patient."

They finished eating and went into the living area, sitting down. It began to get a little chilly, so Caleb got the fire started. Geneva scoped the entire room, memorizing every inch of it, should she ever lose her way again. Then her eyes landed above, on the mantle, where a cross sat front and center.

"I love that cross," she said, putting her hands up to her chest.

"Oh," Elijah said, getting up as quickly as he could. "I have something for you."

Geneva watched him as he treated upstairs, "What in tarnation's is he talkin' 'bout young'uns? I didn't think he had that much Getty up and go in him anymore. Must be important."

They didn't say anything, but Ella and Caleb were pretty sure they knew what he was going to get, at least they thought they knew.

CHAPTER TWENTY-FIVE

The sound of his footsteps coming back down was heard clearly and their eyes were in his direction. He came around the corner with his hands behind his back, carrying the most secretive look across his aging face.

"Whatcha got there?" she asked, reaching around him playfully.

Elijah got down on his knees in front of her, "You see Geneva, we were at this little antique place a bit ago and I found something that reminded me of you, so I had to buy it. I didn't know I'd see you again, but if I had this, I had you in a way. So, close your eyes."

"Doggone it, Elijah, you know I don't do surprises," she said, her stubborn nature shining.

"Stop being contrary woman," he said, aggravating, knowing it would get a rise out of her.

"What'd you say to me?" she continued to banter.

"Please," he asked.

She gave him that look and attitude, but she did as he asked. He took her hand and placed the cross in her hand, "Open your eyes."

Geneva did as he asked, opened her eyes and her hand. That's when she started crying. Her tears were like a hundred rivers making their path down her beautiful face, and her ice-blue eyes shined with disbelief and amazement. She held onto that cross like her life depended on it, then looked up.

"How...where?" she muttered in a confused manner, beginning to shake.

"What do you mean?" he asked, confused why she was so emotional.

Her fingers run over every inch of the cross, feeling each fine line of etchings within it and the beautiful smooth turquoise cross in the middle, and she let out a sigh of relief.

She handed it back to Elijah, and said, "Turn it over Elijah, and you'll understand."

He took it from her, and doing so, he saw something amazing. Etched in the leather on the back, was written, *GENEVA'S CROSS.* Then his mind traveled back to the first moment he ever saw her with the cross. He could still envision her holding it tight to her chest for protection.

"I thought I'd lost it a long time ago," she said. "My grandfather said it wasn't worth anything anyway. He said it was wishful thinkin' that some ole cross could save anybody from anything."

"Wait a minute," Elijah said. "The lady we bought it from said she remembered the man who sold it to her years ago. She said he was a rude sort and just wanted the money and didn't see it important at all."

"He took it and sold it?" Geneva asked, not really in disbelief because he was never a nice person, but more from the shock it had been found.

"I never looked on the back. When I bought it, I just put it in the nightstand by the bed and that's where it's been since, until now," Elijah said.

"It found its way back to me and so did you all," she said. "Do you understand what it all means honey?"

"I understand now," he smiled. "Like you told me years ago, this cross is a symbol telling us all that God's got us. I never believed it before, and it took all these years of anger and hatred to find it. I'm so sorry it took me so long."

They all came close together, putting their hands on that incredible cross, one that traveled through time to find its way back where it belonged.

Geneva smiled and closed her eyes, "The good book says in Luke 14: 27 *Whoever does not carry his own cross and come after Me cannot be My disciple.* I always carried my cross, but now it's carryin' us all."

Her spiritual words were absorbed instantaneously by Elijah, just like when brother Todd read such verses and he had a confession for her.

"Geneva," Elijah said, lovingly holding her hand. "Before we found you, I found myself."

She tilted her head, trying to figure out what he was talking about, and she didn't interrupt, only listened, knowing he had more to say.

"We went to your cowboy church not long ago, and…"

"And…and…don't ya stop there, you done piqued my curiosity, Elijah," Geneva said, trying to pull it out of him.

He let a moment pass, never losing eye contact, then he finished, "I always told you God didn't know who I was… well, now I know that's not the case. Truth was, I didn't know him, but I do now. Brother Todd sure does have a way of preachin' don't he?"

Enthusiasm poured out of her, covering Elijah with hugs and kisses and a bunch of her country slang, most didn't know what it meant. All to say, her happiness radiated all around her, filling every inch of the room.

Just as Elijah on the day he gave his life to the Lord, Geneva's eyes filled with tears overflowing, like a raging river headed to calm waters. Just like Elijah, they were tears of joy, not sadness.

"We goin' to church Sunday?" Geneva asked, as many times before, but this time it was different.

"I wouldn't miss it mama G," he replied, aggravating at the same time.

"I guess you know all my secrets now talkin' to my folks over there. Oh, well," she laughed, showing her joy.

The next few days flew by, Elijah giving Geneva his undivided attention. From doing his best to fix meals, to waiting on her hand and foot, he did everything he could for her. Ella and Caleb stayed and helped to make sure they were okay, but Jimmy, Brenda, and the others had to go home. When Sunday morning rolled around, everyone got up, ate a grand breakfast, and headed to church. Geneva wanted to surprise everyone, so she didn't call anyone to tip them off she would be there on that fine Sunday morning.

"I can't wait to see the looks on their faces, by golly," she said, just down the road from the church. "Oh boy I missed these folks. They're my family too."

Pulling up and parking in the same spot as before, Elijah went around and opened the car door for Geneva. She was sporting her jeans with hints of sparkle on them, carrying her purse with a big rhinestone cross dead in the center and a shiny bolo necklace matching her attire. The minute she stepped out and the first person who saw her, began to call out.

"It's Geneva," the lady said, running over to her with open arms.

Instantly, Geneva was swarmed by people who looked up to her and admired her. Elijah just sat back and stared at the exceptional smile showing across Geneva's face. She hugged everyone boldly, squeezing each one as tight as the one before, then they all walked to the front door. There was laughter, tears, and everything in between. Seeing her with them, completed the picture of who his wife truly was...a woman of God, and finally, they were a perfect match.

"Looks like I'm some sorta celebrity...hehe. Sure, is good to see everybody," she said, steadily running into people who thought they would never see her again.

The energy in that church went to a new level with their Geneva, mama G, back, and during the sermon, she pulled out her worn-out bible and flipped through those pages like a pro. Elijah took in every word, storing it all and trying to learn from such a service, and when it was over, brother Todd, before praying the final prayer, went down the far steps.

Ella slipped Elijah a small duffle bag and everyone watched the preacher as he made his way to the right of the stage, rolling up his sleeves as he walked.

Brother Todd announced, "We have a special treat this morning. We have a baptism. This person has struggled for a long time with his own demons, but he called me up and said he accepted Jesus Christ as his Lord and Savior and wanted to share his decision publicly as it is written. Would you please come on up here Elijah James?"

Elijah got up, kissed Geneva sweetly, grabbed the bag with his extra clothes, and went toward the horse trough where several of the elders stood on either side of it. He stepped in the warm pool of water and did as he was instructed, Geneva following him, then standing against the wall, watching the entire time, tears steadily streaming.

Then brother Todd asked, "Have you accepted Jesus Christ as your Lord and Savior?"

"I have," Elijah said, floods of emotion bursting out.

With hands-on him from both sides, Brother Todd finished, taking him under the water and back up again as he spoke, "I baptize you in the name of the father, the son, and the holy spirit...buried with him in baptism, and raised to walk in a newness of life."

The entire place was filled with clapping, whistling, and a whole lot of amen's, and Geneva handed him a towel when he stepped out. They hugged each other as the final prayer was said and Elijah went in to change clothes.

He got dressed and came out after a few moments, and people were still standing around, visiting and a few were praying with the elders. Towel drying his hair once more so as not to catch his death of a cold walked toward the one person his dreams had focused on, who finally became a reality once again, Geneva.

"I'm so darn proud a you honey," she said, giving him a quick peck on the cheek. "I never woulda believed it... my Elijah, but I never gave up on you. I didn't. I prayed for you when you was being ornery and when you was bein' nice. I bet God got his fill of hearin' your name, but I never stopped."

"You know Geneva," Elijah said. "Remember that night your grandfather was being mean to you, and you told me about what always saved you?"

"Sure honey, I remember."

"I didn't know it then, but it would end up saving me too. From our first real conversation, it's always been there," Elijah smiled.

"What are you talkin' about?" she said, a bit confused.

Elijah, knowing exactly where it was, reached in the side pocket of her purse and pulled out the old leather and turquoise treasure, and said, "This cross," running his fingers over it as he did when he first found it in that little shop near Hot Springs. "It saved you, so you could save me."

"Oh honey," she said. "I didn't save you...God did."

Together, they walked out of that holy place, and there was a new life to look forward to. He took the cross from her hand and held it up to his heart as she always did when she was young, then glanced up at the Heaven's above. Somehow, he knew his life would be different from that day forward, and he muttered where only Heaven could hear, "*Thank you God for Geneva's Cross.*"

Matthew 16; 25 – 26 "Then Jesus said to His disciples, if anyone wishes to come after Me, he must deny himself, and take up his cross and follow Me." AMEN

About the Author

With a passion for words since she was a little girl, Tammy D. Thompson started with writing poetry. Her mother would find little writings around the house and put them up for keeps. As the years passed, and she attended college at Southern Arkansas University in Magnolia, AR, her verses changes into fiction, starting with her first book, *Buried, But Not Forgotten*. As it does, things changed once more, and her books turned into Christian Inspirational books, with the hopes to leave a smile on the reader's face and hope in their hearts. After the *Dream Mountain* Series and her last book, *The Beggar*, Mrs. Thompson's goal was to relay a message in every story she wrote. In her most recent title, *Geneva's Cross*, and the Geneva book series to come, the message is very clear. Throughout many changes in her life, the one constant was always God and his love for her. So, in this latest series, each book is meant to lead and direct the reader in the direction of the light and away from any darkness. "At the end of the day, I want to touch hearts and changes lives," Mrs. Thompson said. "There's nothing more rewarding than knowing you made a difference in even one person's life. And that's my goal as a writer, as a person, and as a Christian." One of her favorite scriptures is Mark 11:23 *"Therefore I tell you, whatever you ask for in prayer, believe that you have received it, and it will be yours."* She does everything through her faith and her hope is to convey every ounce of that faith to her readers, praying it is received in the way it is given. Using her gift of words, she wants to change the world, one person at a time. You can keep up with Tammy's books on her website at www.TammyDThompson.com.